ALSO BY RICKY FRY

He Comes in the Night

Lionshead

Bill and Ty Get High

YOU ARE MINE

RICKY FRY

VERTIGO PRESS

For Mom, who is always the first to read my books.

YOU
ARE
MINE

PROLOGUE

Fourteen days. That's how long I've been trapped in the basement of this monster's cabin. I only know because I've been scratching lines into the moldy concrete walls of my cage with a metal bolt on the shackles around my wrists, watching as the sun rises and sets beyond a tiny window high in the wall. Sometimes, in the long, dark hours of my captivity, I imagine I'm small enough to crawl through that window, slither right between those rusty bars and disappear like some tiny creature into the forest.

At least, I think there's a forest. The truth is, I don't even know which state I'm in. Maybe Utah, or Colorado, or Wyoming. When I close my eyes at night and listen carefully, I can hear the hooting of a nearby owl and sometimes the distant howling of a coyote.

He thinks I'm starting to love him. That's why he brought me here. He says he loves me, and if he keeps me here long enough, I'll love him too. At first, I'd bite and claw and spit, but now I go along with it. Maybe if he thinks it's true that I really do love him, he'll take off the chains and let me out of his dungeon. Then I could run. It doesn't even matter if I die. I just want to feel that one thing we all take for granted until we don't have it. Freedom.

Fourteen days. That's how long I've been trapped in the basement of this monster's cabin.

My name is Spencer Madison. I'm twenty-three years old. This is my story.

ONE

I was tired. More than tired—exhausted. The kind of deep exhaustion that sinks into your bones and robs you of the will to live. I'd been driving for nearly two days straight, stopping only long enough for a few hours of sleep at a roadside rest stop.

I was somewhere east of the Colorado Rockies, but where I was exactly, I couldn't be sure. The road was a straight line extending out for miles over the empty horizon, hemmed in only by the hypnotic glow of lane markers reflecting in the car's high-beam headlights.

Keep driving. It was what I'd told myself over and over since I'd fled Portland in a panic. *Keep driving.* If only my eyelids weren't so heavy.

A rumble beneath the tires sent a shot of adrenaline pumping through my veins. My eyes snapped wide open just in time to jerk the wheel back to the left and avoid drifting off the road.

That was close—too close.

The surge of adrenaline had almost passed when the dark space of the car's interior was flooded with the blue and red lights of a police cruiser.

I worked to steady myself as I brought the car to a stop along the shoulder, hands shaking despite my tight grip on the wheel. *Deep breath. That's it. Now take another. They don't know anything, not all the way out here.*

"Good evening, miss." The officer touched the tip of his hat. "My name is Trooper Evans with the Kansas Highway Patrol. Do you know why I pulled you over?"

I squinted in the bright beam of his flashlight. "I'm sorry, officer. I'm just a little sleepy. It's been a long drive."

"You come all the way from Oregon?"

My heart skipped a beat. How did he know where I was from? Then I remembered the Oregon license plates. They were hard to forget. Matt had waited a month for his custom vanity plates to arrive in the mail. I'd tried to convince him otherwise, but he'd insisted on his first choice: ISELL4U. Now, almost forty-eight hours into my escape, I wished he'd gone with something more subtle.

I nodded.

"That's a long way to be traveling alone." The trooper adjusted his shoulders the way all police officers do when they're mulling something over. "Where you headed?"

"St. Louis."

"You got family there?"

"It's my mom," I said. "She's sick—cancer." It was only half a lie. My mom did have cancer. But she'd died almost ten years before. I hoped she'd forgive me for the lie, wherever she might be.

"I'm sorry to hear that. Listen, there's another rest stop just a few miles up the road. Real nice. It's got bright lights and a security patrol to keep the creeps away. Why don't you pull over and get some sleep? I can follow behind, make sure you get there okay."

"Thank you, officer. It's just—I'm in a real hurry to get to St. Louis."

"You'll be no use to anyone, least of all to your mother, if you crash and wind up dead."

Dead. That's exactly what I'd be if Matt caught up to me. Still, I thought it best to go along with what the trooper was saying. I didn't want him asking any more questions—didn't want him discovering what I was really doing so far from home. Besides, I told myself I could always leave the rest stop after he pulled away.

"Yes," I said, nodding again. "You're right."

He lowered the flashlight and smiled. "Great. Just a quick check of your license and registration, and we'll have you on your way."

Fuck. I swallowed hard and forced a thin smile across my face. "Registration?"

"Standard procedure."

"Oh, of course." I fumbled around in the glove box until I found the slip of paper with Matt's name on it.

The trooper frowned as he inspected it. "I don't suppose you're Matt?"

"He's my fiancé." That part was true. He'd proposed on Valentine's Day, exactly six months after we'd first started dating. It was a bit too cheesy for my taste, but Matt was like that. He'd always been a hopeless romantic. Always the perfect gentleman. Looking back on things, I couldn't believe how easily I'd missed the warning signs. They were there all along—hidden in plain sight—insults disguised as compliments, jealous questions about where I'd been, and who I was with.

"And this Matt, I'm going to assume he gave you permission to use his vehicle?"

I nodded for the third time. *Keep it simple. Stay calm. Don't slip up.*

"Must be a real big shot."

It was the last part that caught me off guard. I forced another awkward smile as my mind raced to make sense of what he'd said. "Big shot?"

"Hey, it's none of my business, but if my fiancé was driving halfway across the country to visit her sick mother, I'd make time in my schedule to come along."

It's those stupid license plates. Even Matt's friends at the real estate agency had teased him about them—said they made him look like an asshole. *They were right.*

"He's flying out on Tuesday." This wasn't the first time I'd lied to a police officer. The tricky part was giving them just enough details to satisfy their stubborn curiosity without giving anything away. "I decided not to wait."

"Fair enough. Now, how about that driver's license?"

"Yes, just one second." I made a small show of fumbling around in search of my license, though I already knew I'd left it behind in Portland. "I'm sorry, officer. I can't seem to find it."

The trooper released a heavy sigh as he produced a small notepad from his shirt pocket. "Okay," he said. "I'll need you to spell your name for me. And your date of birth, I'm going to need that too."

"Felicity Hoffman. F—E—L—I—" I recited each letter carefully before moving on to the last name. The date of birth came just as easily. Felicity had been my best friend since high school, and we had a small tradition of celebrating her birthday with an annual weekend trip to the Pacific Coast.

Felicity would forgive me for using her name, especially after what had happened with Matt.

"Wait here," said the officer.

I watched him saunter back to his cruiser and hoped the lie would hold up. I couldn't risk using my real name, not with a previous conviction on my record.

I fumbled with the radio as I waited. It was a welcome distraction, but the only two channels I could find were country music and a preacher going on about the sins of pornography. I hated country music almost as much as I hated preachers.

Twenty minutes passed. Then thirty. I fidgeted in my seat. *What was taking so long?* I wondered if they had a photo of a smiling Felicity in their database. Had they discovered I wasn't really who I'd claimed to be?

I bit the inside of my lip and tasted blood. If only I hadn't been in such a hurry to leave Portland, I might have remembered to bring the pills my doctor at the community health center had recently prescribed for anxiety.

My spinning thoughts were interrupted by the bright headlights of another vehicle approaching from the opposite direction. I watched as it passed—a second police cruiser, shiny decals reflecting in the bouncing lights of the trooper's car. It made a wide turn, tires grinding on the asphalt, and swung into place behind the first.

One police officer was bad enough. Two was a complete disaster.

Minutes before, my thoughts had been swimming, threatening to drown me, but now a single thought burned brightly in my mind. *Run.*

The trooper's voice was no longer friendly as it boomed from a loudspeaker. I could see him in the rear-view mirror, crouched down behind an open door with a microphone raised to his lips. "Shut off the ignition," he said in a commanding tone. "Step out of the vehicle with your hands in the air."

It was the moment I'd feared since grabbing Matt's keys and backing out of the driveway. There was only one thing I knew for certain. I could never go back to Portland, not unless I wanted to die.

Screw it. I shifted the Audi into drive and slammed my foot down hard on the accelerator, a cloud of dust and gravel spitting up from the car's tires as they spun and found their grip on the asphalt. *Too late for second guesses.*

The speedometer climbed past ninety. Then one-hundred. And as I saw the trooper's headlights fade away in the rear-view mirror, I felt more alive than I'd felt in all the months since I'd become engaged to Matt.

I felt scared too, but for one brief second, I threw my head back and laughed. That's when I saw the headlights reappear in the rear-view mirror, closing the distance as quickly as I'd put it between us.

I remembered a movie I'd seen once, something about the police not crossing state lines. I couldn't remember the name of the movie, but I knew it starred Burt Reynolds. My mom had always loved Burt Reynolds. In the movie, he'd played some kind of criminal on the run, who only had to cross the state line to get away clean. I wondered if it were really true, and if so, how close the nearest state line might be.

The speedometer broke a hundred and ten. Then a hundred and twenty.

I was too high on adrenaline and too busy watching the red and blue lights behind me to notice the deer bounding across the highway. The last thing I saw, before the windshield blew out with a violent crash, was the poor creature's eyes glowing green in the dark as the hood of Matt's Audi struck flesh.

TWO

Pain. Before I'd even opened my eyes, the only thing I felt was pain. Too much pain to know where I was or how I got there. *Oh, right, the accident.*

For a moment, I thought I might be dead. No, there was too much pain to be dead.

I managed a squint. A white room. White bed. I was in the hospital. At least it looked like a hospital. Light poured in from an open window and bore into my skull. I tried to raise my hand to shield my eyes and was surprised when it would move no more than a few inches. Stainless steel wrapped itself tightly around my wrist. I was handcuffed to the bed frame on both sides, and when I looked down, there were matching shackles around my ankles.

Panic hit me hard. I'd always been afraid of confined spaces and the loss of movement. Once, Matt had suggested some light bondage to spice things up in the bedroom. Just the thought of it had sent my head spinning. Now, as I thrashed wildly on the bed, I was reminded of a recurring dream I'd had as a little girl. Night after night, I'd find myself buried alive in a tight wooden box, fingernails ripping from bloodied flesh as I fought to scratch and claw my way to freedom.

"Take it easy," said a young man in green hospital scrubs. He wore a friendly look on his face and flashed me a pearly smile. "You're pretty banged up—don't want to make it worse."

I'd been too busy struggling against the handcuffs to notice him entering the room. He couldn't have been much older than I was, and something about his presence calmed my crackling nerves. "Where am I?"

"The hospital," he said.

I released a long sigh and felt my muscles relaxing as I eased back into the mattress. "Yes, I know I'm in the hospital. But *where* am I?"

His lips parted to reveal another smile. "You must've really taken a hit." His arms widened, and gestured around the room. "Topeka. You're in Topeka, Kansas, home of pentecostalism and Brown v. Board of Education."

Fucking Kansas. It was the last place a girl from Oregon expected to wind up shackled to a hospital bed.

"Hey, you need anything? You've been asleep since they brought you in."

"You got a joint?" The words came out of my mouth without thought, and I was surprised to find my sense of humor hadn't abandoned me.

He laughed. "I did mention you're in Kansas, right? How about some water? That's still legal, at least it was the last time I checked."

The mere mention of water made me realize how dry and scratchy my throat was. It was like I hadn't had anything to drink for days. "Thanks. Water's great."

He ducked out of the room and returned a minute later, carrying a plastic serving tray with a small pitcher and a matching plastic cup. I thought he might sit on the bed beside me, but instead, he remained standing, close enough to raise the cup to my lips but far enough away to maintain a professional distance.

I took a sip and read the name on the ID badge hanging from the pocket of his scrub shirt. "Alexander Martinez, RN. You're a nurse?"

He nodded. "You can call me Alex."

"Well, Alex, as much as I love the personal service, things would be a lot easier if you took off these handcuffs. I'm sure you have much more important things to do than babysit me."

There was the sound of metal clinking as I raised my hands a few inches and then lowered them back down to my sides.

"No can do," he said. "It's a police matter."

I gave him my best smile, despite the throbbing pain still beating inside my head. "I promise I won't cause any trouble."

"Look, it's my job to help people. I don't judge, and I'm sure you're a nice person. But I couldn't take those things off even if I wanted to. They don't give me the keys."

Damn. With the handcuffs off, I might have been able to make a break for it, though I had no idea where the car was or if it was even still drivable. Alex was friendly, but he wasn't as gullible as I might have hoped. And there was still the problem of the shackles around my ankles.

"What if I have to pee?"

He laughed again, a gentle chuckle that formed soft creases at the corners of his eyes. "Go right ahead. We inserted a catheter when they brought you in last night. I've already emptied it twice."

I tried not to imagine the bag of yellow liquid between my legs or the young man who was now serving me water coming back later to empty it. "What did they say?"

"Huh?"

"The police. What did they say when they brought me in?"

As if on cue, the door swung open. A stiff man in uniform, the same one who'd first pulled me over, entered the room along with a middle-aged woman in a suit.

The woman's lips pulled back into a tight smile. "Good afternoon," she said. "I'm Deputy District Attorney Collins. I believe you already know Trooper Evans."

I reverted back to nodding, waiting to see what they had to say before opening my mouth. The young nurse had been a welcome distraction, but now, with an officer in uniform hovering near the bed, I was reminded once again of the handcuffs secured tightly around my wrists.

Collins continued. "Do you remember what happened last night?"

I shook my head. "It's all a bit foggy." Another lie. I would never forget the frightened look in that poor creature's eyes before it smashed headfirst into the windshield. "Am I under arrest?"

It was the deputy district attorney's turn to nod. "Yes, I'm afraid you've been charged with evading and resisting arrest, reckless driving, and a host of additional traffic violations."

The room spun, and I thought I might get sick. *It's okay. Hold steady. They still don't know about Portland. About Matt.* Maybe I'd get off with a ticket or some community service—anything to get me back on the road and far away from Oregon. I stared down at the chain between my ankles. *A ticket might be hoping for too much.*

When I looked back up, the trooper was glaring at me through narrowed eyes, his hands fidgeting with the heavy buckle on his belt. "If I were you," he said in a voice that reminded me of my dead father, "I'd consider myself lucky to be alive. Just last week, a family of four was killed in a similar crash, and they weren't going nearly so fast."

Should I apologize? No, an apology was an admission of guilt. "What happens next?"

Collins frowned as she removed a pair of reading glasses from her suit pocket and pushed them up her narrow nose. Then she opened a folder she'd been carrying in her left hand and studied the contents as if reading them for the first time. "Ordinarily, we'd prosecute vigorously and seek the maximum allowable punishment under Kansas law."

But? Please tell me there's a but?

"But, due to complicating factors, we've decided not to prosecute your case."

Trooper Evans muttered something under his breath.

I would have leaped right off the bed if I hadn't been handcuffed to it. *Was the car totaled?* No matter, I would settle for the next bus heading east out of Kansas. I turned my attention back to Trooper Evans, expecting him to saunter over with that sour look on his face and release me from the cuffs. *What was taking him so long?*

Collins cleared her throat. "Make no mistake, I'd certainly be happy to prosecute, and I believe I'd secure a conviction. Trooper Evans wrote quite the report. But it's not in the best interests of Kansas taxpayers to incarcerate you for these relatively minor offenses, not with such serious charges pending against you in Oregon."

Trooper Evans' face curled into a tight-lipped smile.

"Oregon?"

"Yes," said Collins. "Turns out the car you were driving is stolen."

Matt. Of course, it was Matt. He must have reported the car stolen the moment he'd found it missing from the driveway.

Whatever small measure of freedom I'd felt during the last two days on the road was slipping through my fingers. If only they knew the truth about what had really happened the night I fled Oregon. "Stolen? That's impossible. There must be some kind of mistake."

Collins waved a sheet of paper with some kind of computer printout. "No mistake," she said. "Though I'm afraid a stolen vehicle is the least of your concerns. The driver is wanted for attempted murder."

Attempted murder? The words filled the room and settled in my brain, somewhere alongside the pain still pulsing between my temples. "What? That's impossible. You must have the wrong information."

"I'm afraid not," said Collins. "Now, why don't you start by telling us who you really are."

THREE

Two deputies sat me down across the metal table from a man in a cheap, wrinkled business suit. The rough fabric of the orange jumpsuit I'd been issued scratched at my skin.

Trooper Evans had brought me from the hospital straight to the county jail just as soon as the doctors had signed off on my health. It was an experience I'd never forget—the chain between my ankles clinking loudly as I was shuffled through the emergency room and out to his waiting patrol car. But it was the gawks and stares, people seated in rows of plastic chairs averting their eyes while silently judging me, that would stay burned forever in my memory.

"My name is Andrew," said the man in the cheap suit. "Andrew Smith. I've been sent by the court to represent you." He offered his hand, and I shook it.

I'd requested a lawyer the moment Collins had sprung the attempted murder charge on me in the hospital. I'd watched enough television to know talking to the police and the prosecutors was never a good thing, no matter how hard they tried to convince you otherwise.

The lawyer smiled, revealing thin lines around his tired eyes. "Do you need anything? Water? Coffee? There's a vending machine out in the hallway, and I'd be happy to buy you a soda."

"No," I said. "I'm fine." I'd had lunch in the jail cafeteria not long before they escorted me into the room to meet with the lawyer. The lunch had been awful—a thin slice of cheese and some kind of processed mystery meat between two pieces of dry bread—but the company of misfit characters seated around me at the table had almost made up for the poor quality of the food.

"Very well." He opened a worn leather shoulder bag and flipped through a thick stack of folders until he found one with my name scribbled on it in black marker. "I've reviewed the details of your case, and well, I won't sugarcoat things. It's not looking good."

What does that mean? I'd spent the previous night in a narrow cell, holding out some kind of hope that it was all just a terrible misunderstanding. I'd even allowed myself to imagine the lawyer telling me I was free to leave. It was all so clear in my head. I'd change back into my black hoodie and matching Chuck Taylors, catch a bus to the nearest on-ramp, and hitch a ride out of town. Now, as I stared back at him from across the table, the expression on the lawyer's face told me it wasn't going to be so easy.

He waited for me to speak, and when it was clear I wasn't going to say anything, he continued. "Spencer—do you mind if I call you Spencer?"

I shrugged my shoulders. The police had confirmed my identity after the fingerprints they took at the jail matched a shoplifting charge I'd picked up at sixteen. It was the one, and only other time I'd found myself in a jail cell, and that had only been a few hours in juvie before my foster parents came to bail me out.

The lawyer glanced down at his folder and then back up to me. "Well, Spencer, you've been charged back in Oregon with stealing your boyfriend's Audi. He's also saying you tried to kill him."

I couldn't hold my silence any longer. "Matt said that?"

The lawyer nodded.

Go figure. It was just like him to cover his tracks, especially when it had really been Matt who'd tried to kill me. "But that's not what happened."

The lawyer took a photo from the folder and slid it across the smooth metal table. In it, Matt was lying on a hospital bed with a row of staples holding a large gash on his forehead together. It made me sick to my stomach just to see him, and it had nothing to do with the blood.

"He's a liar," I said.

"Perhaps," said the lawyer, "but that wound was enough to convince the police and DA's office in Portland to file the charges. It certainly doesn't help you were caught five states over in his Audi."

"Please, I was only defending myself. You have to help me. Matt was trying—"

He raised a hand. "Even if I wanted to help, and I do, the charges are in Oregon. This is Kansas, and the State of Kansas has declined to file any charges for the accident."

"So, what happens now?"

"Well, they'll hold an extradition hearing and then ship you back to Portland. I'm only here to represent you during the hearing. You're going to need another lawyer when you get back to Oregon, preferably a very, very good one."

Ship me back to Portland? I couldn't believe what I was hearing. Portland was the last place I wanted to end up. Sure, it had been home all my life. But Matt was there, and I didn't want to be anywhere near him. "What about the hearing? Isn't there something you can do?"

"I can file a motion to stay the extradition. But I'm afraid that would only buy you some time. That's assuming the judge even considers the motion, which, if I'm honest, Spencer, isn't very likely. Kansas likes to move things along quickly in these matters. Until then, you're just another prisoner eating food at the taxpayer's expense."

I buried my head in my hands, and for the first time since peeling out of the driveway in Matt's Audi, I felt the overwhelming urge to cry. No, I told myself. Not in this place. But it was no use. Big, sloppy tears ran down my cheeks and wet the orange sleeves of my jumpsuit.

"I'm sorry," he said.

I was still crying when the deputies came to take me away.

The hearing came and went. As expected, the judge ordered my immediate extradition to the State of Oregon. Less than two weeks after I'd arrived in Kansas, I was escorted from my cell by two more deputies to a holding area I recognized from when Trooper Evans had brought me over from the hospital.

That's when I first saw him. He was young, close to my own age, and wore a different uniform than the deputies who worked the jail.

The deputies handed him a file, and he inspected it, glancing up at me for a moment as if he might be studying me the way a scientist studies a slide in a microscope. If I had known what was to come, I would have screamed and spit and punched one of the deputies so they'd have to hold me in Kansas on more charges. But we never really know what's to come until it's already come to pass.

"Spencer Madison?" He smiled as he said my name.

I nodded.

"I need you to say yes or no. Say it aloud. Are you Spencer Madison?"

"Yes."

"Great," he said. "I'm your ride to Portland. My name is Travis." He motioned over his shoulder to a woman in a black uniform that matched his own. "This is Monica."

"Um, okay." *Is he expecting me to say it's nice to meet him?*

The deputies took me into a side room and instructed me to change out of the orange jumpsuit. Then they gave me a matching set of bright pink prisoner scrubs marked in large block letters: CORRECTIONAL TRANSPORT COMPANY OF AMERICA.

When I'd changed, they brought me back to the holding area, where Travis and a deputy were taking an inventory of my personal items. Black hoodie. Black Converse Chuck

Taylors. I should have been happy, or at least felt some comfort, to see my things. But instead, it was only a sad reminder of my situation. I doubted I'd be wearing my own clothes again for a long time.

Travis handed the clear plastic bag to his partner and motioned me over to a concrete bench. "Kneel down on the bench with your legs out behind you."

Reluctantly, I did as I was told. I knew what would come next—it was the same when they'd taken me to the courthouse—though it didn't stop the butterflies in my stomach when he snapped the rigid metal shackles around my ankles.

"I'm sorry," he said. "They've got to be tight. It's in the regulations. But I'll leave a little wiggle room for you."

Great. Now he wants me to thank him like he's doing me some kind of favor.

He helped me down from the bench—hot, sweaty hands gripping my shoulders, and then instructed me to raise my arms out to my sides. I stood silently as he put a chain around my waist and cuffed my hands in front.

Monica signed some paperwork, and they led me out to a white van marked with the same block letters as the pink uniform they'd issued me. I was relieved to see two more female prisoners in the back of the van and even more relieved when it was Monica, and not Travis, who reached across my lap to buckle the seatbelt.

When she was satisfied my seatbelt was secure, Monica, who hadn't spoken a single word to me, climbed into the passenger seat up front—they were separated from us by a heavy wire cage—while Travis made a show of checking the tires before sliding into the driver's seat and adjusting the mirrors.

"Safety first," he said with an eager tone, as though we were one big happy family on a road trip.

Yeah. The road trip from hell.

FOUR

"What's your name?" said a quiet, mousy voice from the seat behind me.

We'd been riding in silence for nearly an hour. Well, almost silence. Monica had tuned the radio to a country music station and was happily humming along to some guy singing about his pickup truck.

It's almost like she knows how much I hate country music.

I twisted around to catch a glimpse of the young woman who'd broken the impasse, struggling against the seatbelt and the handcuffs chained to my waist. I wasn't sure if I even wanted a conversation or if the guards would allow it, but it was better than passing the time thinking of Matt.

"Spencer," I said. "My name is Spencer."

"Cool name. I'm Ruby. You know, like the gemstone. My grandmother says they named me Ruby because of how red my skin was when I was born."

She wore a thick pair of black glasses that made her slender, freckled face appear delicate. Almost fragile.

"I'd shake your hand, Ruby, but—"

She laughed, a sort of half giggle with a snort, and I decided right away that I liked her.

"So," she said, "what's your story?"

"My story?"

"Yeah, what'd you do to end up stuffed in the back of this van?"

"Nothing."

She laughed and snorted again. "Oh, come on. We all did something. Me? I drove from Washington to a music festival in Atlanta with sixteen pounds of psilocybin mushrooms in my camper van. Would have made it too, if my dumbass boyfriend hadn't fallen asleep and crashed the van just fifty miles from the festival."

"Wow." I was surprised by her confession. Ruby looked more like the kind of girl who'd sell muffins at a counter in some indie bookstore than an interstate drug smuggler.

"They're not drugs," she said as if somehow reading my mind. "They're medicine. There's powerful healing in those mushrooms. Have you ever tried?"

"Shrooms? No, but I don't think people should go to jail for it."

"Tell that to the feds." Another snort. "So I've told you my story. What's yours?"

I looked up just in time to see the curious grin on Travis' face as he watched us in the rear-view mirror. Monica appeared entirely uninterested and reached for the radio dial to turn the music up a notch or two.

"It's all just a misunderstanding. I'm sure they'll figure it out when I get back to Oregon." It was more than just an excuse not to explain the details. I still clung to some hope that my problems would somehow go away when I had a chance to tell my side of the story.

"Look," she said, "I won't tell anyone. And those guards up front aren't cops."

"They're not?"

"Nope. Correctional Transport Company of America is a private company. They stuff people into vans just like this one and drive them all over the country—make a big profit by billing the states and paying the guards shit. I read an article about it once on Vice. And now here I am, just another part of the story."

"Is that legal?"

Travis, who must have been eavesdropping on our conversation, jumped in. "Legal as sin. Hell, they're traded on the stock exchange. The rich keep getting richer, while Monica and I make a cool twelve dollars an hour driving seventy-two-hour runs."

Monica groaned. "Travis—"

He waved her off. "But that doesn't mean I don't take my job seriously. You might think I'm only here to drive you from jail to jail like I'm some kind of bad guy. Truth is, I'm here to keep you safe. When you're in my custody, you're my responsibility, and I'm not gonna let anything bad happen to you."

He winked at me in the rear-view mirror, and a shiver traveled down my spine. I couldn't say why he gave me the creeps. It seemed like he was only being nice, just another young guy working a job like anyone else. He was certainly more pleasant than Monica.

"Okay, let's hear it," said Ruby. "Tell us your story."

"Go on," said Travis, winking at me again. "It's not like I haven't already read the charges in your file."

"Well—" I hesitated for a moment, unsure if it was wise to continue. "They said I tried to murder my fiancé."

"Damn." Ruby whistled. "I had no idea you were such a badass."

I was still surprised to hear that kind of language coming from her thin lips. "It's not true. I never tried to kill anyone. I hit him over the head with a model home—some stupid mockup for a bland development he was selling—and it was self-defense."

"Sure thing, honey." It was the older woman on the seat behind Ruby who spoke, her voice low and gravelly like someone who'd been smoking two packs a day for fifty years. "With men, it's always self-defense. Your only mistake was not killing the bastard."

"That's Denise," said Ruby. "She—"

"I can speak for myself," said the older woman. "Killed my husband twenty-three years ago. Cut his body up into little pieces and fed it to the pigs. He had it coming too. Always getting drunk and slapping me around. You know something? I ain't never had a single regret. Only got caught now because of that new DNA evidence. I'm surprised anyone still cared."

I wondered if that would have been my life in twenty years if I'd stayed put and married Matt. He wasn't a heavy drinker, and he'd never hit me. His own brand of torture was something different, something much more suffocating and controlling than a slap in the face.

"Isn't this great?" Ruby was awfully perky for someone facing federal drug charges. "I've always wanted friends to share secrets with."

Monica grumbled from the front seat. "Yeah, you guys are just like the Sisterhood of the Traveling Pants."

I smiled to myself. *Even though we're in chains, Monica is the most miserable one in this van.*

When I looked up, Travis was smiling too. Another wink in the rear-view mirror. Another shiver down my spine.

FIVE

Any girl will tell you peeing in a gas station bathroom is never easy. The piss on the seat. Tampon wrappers on the floor. It's even harder when you're in shackles.

"One hand," said Monica as she shuffled us one after the other from the van into the filthy bathroom, chains clinking between our ankles with each restricted step. "I'll unlock one hand, so you can wipe."

Thanks, Monica. You're such an angel.

I'd had to pee since about two hours into the journey, but Monica said I had to hold it until we reached one of the approved stops along our route. I wasn't eager to be paraded around the parking lot in chains, but my need to pee overwhelmed my shame. I even smiled at an older couple fueling up their RV, mortified looks of horror and contempt on their faces.

Oh, come on. It's not like we actually murdered someone. Okay, maybe Denise killed her husband, but that was twenty-three years ago. And according to her, he deserved it.

By now, we were four hours into our trip, and I was starting to wonder how long the journey back to Oregon would take. The limited freedom of a jail cell was beginning to look good compared to being shackled in the back of a van. At least I could stretch my arms in a jail cell.

Travis fueled the van and checked the tires again. I had to admit I appreciated his commitment to safety, even if it came off as that sort of protective male bravado most Portland girls like me do our best to ignore.

When he was satisfied the van was in order, Monica climbed into the driver's seat for her shift behind the wheel.

Four hours. Fours hours, and we're still in fucking Kansas.

It was another two hours to the state line. A sign welcomed us to "Colorful Colorado," and I closed my eyes, imagining for a moment I was on a trip with my friends and would soon be smoking Rocky Mountain weed.

"Do you think we'll see it?" Ruby's squeaky voice interrupted my fantasy.

When I opened my eyes, I was still in the van. "See what?"

"Denver. The Mile High City?"

"I don't know, Ruby. Maybe."

"I've always wanted to go to Denver. Did you know it was voted the best place to live in 2016? The city council decriminalized psilocybin mushrooms in 2019. Maybe I could live there some day—when this is all over."

"That's a nice thought."

"You don't think it could happen?"

"I don't know, Ruby. Two weeks ago, I was drinking a beer in downtown Portland with my friends. Now I'm shackled in the back of a prisoner transport van. Anything can happen."

I'd thought about that night many times in the last two weeks. It was the same night I hit Matt over the head with that stupid model house and burned rubber out of town. I'd come home after the beer to find him pacing the living room in a jealous rage. He was always jealous. At first, I'd found it kind of cute, but as the months passed, he'd become more possessive, more controlling. What he'd said that night had left me with no choice but to run.

"I'm sorry," said Ruby.

"Sorry for what?"

"For bothering you. My grandmother always said I could be a bit too enthusiastic. It's just, other than my boyfriend, I've never really had any friends."

"Do you miss him?"

"Like crazy."

I heard tiny sobs interrupted by a snort coming from Ruby's position in the seat behind me. "I'm sorry too," I said. "You'll get to Denver someday."

"You really think so?"

"Sure, and I'll come for a visit."

"Thank you, Spencer! Oh, thank you so much."

Hope is the only thing keeping her going. Why should I be the one to destroy that?

Thirty minutes after we'd crossed the Colorado state line, Monica pulled the van into a rest stop. More clinking chains between our legs. More balancing over dirty toilet seats with one hand. More obvious stares from families on their way to Mount Rushmore or the Grand Canyon.

I was the last to go, and when I was escorted by Monica's firm grip back to the van, Travis was taking brown paper bags from a long cooler behind the rear doors.

Monica belted us into our seats as Travis passed around the bags along with small, plastic water bottles.

"Eat up," he said, opening his own brown bag as the van pulled back onto the highway.

My cuffed hands fumbled to pull a cheese sandwich and a bruised apple out of the bag. "How am I supposed to eat like this?"

"Not my problem," said Monica.

I bent down as far as the seatbelt would allow and twisted sideways. It wasn't comfortable, but I managed to take a bite of the apple before moving on to the sandwich.

"Hey!" Denise's gravelly old voice barked from the backseat. "How 'bout some real food? I'm sick of the same crappy sandwiches."

Monica's eyes glared back in the rear-view mirror. "We eat the same thing you eat. Stop complaining."

"You know what?" Travis held his sandwich up and then dropped it unceremoniously to the floor. "She's right. There's a McDonald's in Burlington. I'm getting a burger."

"Yeah, you know that's not going to happen." Monica's eyes were back on the road. "We can only make approved stops."

"Screw 'em. We've been driving for two days, Monica. Don't you want a milkshake?"

Denise barked again. "I want a milkshake!"

"Not you guys," he said. "Come on, Monica. At least let me buy you some fries. We'll make it quick."

Monica sighed. "Fine, but it's your ass if we get in trouble."

The line for the drive-through was backed up into the parking lot, car after car of summer road-trippers stopping for milkshakes and hamburgers.

"Park it," said Travis. "I'll run in."

"Are you sure that's a good idea?"

"It'll be fine, Monica. They're in a cage, and the door is locked. What could happen?"

She looked around as though she was expecting to see something. "Alright, just make it quick."

He disappeared into the brown and yellow building, and Monica fidgeted with the steering wheel. None of us said anything. We could sense her unease and knew it was better to keep our mouths shut.

The silence was interrupted by the ringing of a cell phone. Monica jumped in her seat.

She fumbled with the phone for a moment and hesitated before answering. "Lujan speaking ... yes, sir ... I apologize. We should have called in the stop ... yes, everything is fine. Travis thought he heard an odd sound and wanted to check under the hood."

She hung up the phone, and we sat in silence again. Travis returned a few minutes later, carrying a much bigger brown bag and a cardboard drink holder. When he'd climbed in and passed the bag to Monica, he jumped back down and came around to the side of the van. I heard the fumbling of keys before the door swung open.

Monica's hand went to her forehead. "What are you doing?"

He shrugged her off and held out a milkshake. "They must have made a mistake in there, gave us an extra one. You want it, Spencer?"

I could almost feel Denise's eyes burning a hole in the back of my head, but a tall, vanilla milkshake sounded like paradise after two weeks of jail food.

"It's okay," he said. "Take it."

I nodded, and he placed the ice-cold drink between my fingers. There was even a cherry on top.

"Thank you," I said.

Maybe he really is a sweet guy, just stuck doing a job he hates like everyone else.

But as he pulled his hand away from mine, it came to rest, if only for the briefest moment, on my knee. And he winked—that same wink that sent shivers running down my spine—as if he knew a secret I'd soon find out.

SIX

"You know I covered for you back there?" Monica was furious, all that pent up silence exploding in an instant.

"What? How?"

"They called," she said. "When you were busy buying a milkshake for your girlfriend. You're not fooling anyone with that act."

"What did you tell them?"

"Said we heard a funny noise, and you jumped out to check under the hood. They wanted to know why we didn't call it in."

"Did they buy it?"

"I think so."

"Thanks, Monica. I owe you one."

"I can't afford to get fired, Travis. You know my little brother has—"

"—cancer. Yeah, I know. Look, I'm sorry. Okay?"

So there's the truth. Monica isn't angry. She's afraid for her brother and feeling the stress.

The milkshake still cupped in my hands was getting warm. I couldn't take a sip after Travis' hand had found its way to my knee. Maybe it was an accident, and the wink was just an unintentionally creepy habit.

No, I'd been too quick to dismiss the warning signs with Matt until everything had gone terribly wrong. At least, based on the call from company headquarters, I figured the van must have had some kind of GPS tracking unit. I felt a little better knowing someone, somewhere, was keeping an eye on things.

"Hey, aren't you going to drink that?" Travis had spun around in his seat and was looking at me through the wire divider.

"I'm not feeling well. Maybe Ruby could have it." I would have passed it to her myself if my arms weren't pinned down.

The disappointment swelled in his eyes, and his lips moved like he was searching for words. "It was an extra one anyway. It's fine."

I was relieved when he turned around and reached for the radio dial. Even more relieved when he found something other than country music.

"Wake up, Spencer." Ruby's gentle voice coming from behind me stirred me awake. The sun was setting behind distant mountains, and the orange glow of a city rose up before us.

"What? How long was I asleep?"

"About an hour. Isn't it beautiful?"

"Where are we?" I couldn't remember dozing off, but the milkshake still resting between my hands had melted.

"Denver," she said with a tone of wonder in her voice as if we'd somehow found ourselves at the gates of Oz. "Aren't the mountains lovely?"

"You made it."

"Yeah." She laughed and snorted. "I'll get out of the van here, please."

Much to Ruby's delight, we indeed stopped in Denver, arriving at the Downtown Detention Center—a brutalist mid-rise building with mud-brown walls—after nearly an hour of fighting city traffic.

Monica backed the van into a secure garage, and we were allowed to use the bathroom before being belted back into our seats.

"Got a hot one for you," a detention deputy in a dark blue shirt said to Travis. "She's a fighter."

Monica produced another set of bright pink scrubs from the back of the van and followed Travis and the deputy into another room.

I heard the screams before they'd even come back to the garage—a high pitch, bloodcurdling wail you'd expect from someone being murdered.

It took four of them to carry her, one for each arm and leg, suspending her in between them as she thrashed and spit and kicked at her chains.

Monica still had the bright pink scrubs tucked under one arm.

"I told you," said the deputy. "This one's a real mess. Hey, you guys need a spit hood?"

Travis took a fine mess hood from the deputy and cinched it over the girl's head. She was young, maybe even younger than me, with the look in her eyes of some wild beast caught in a hunter's trap.

"Careful," said the deputy. "She's a biter."

Great. I hope they're not planning on putting her next to me.

I was relieved when Monica unfastened my seatbelt and motioned me back a seat. I shuffled my way around, head bent over in the tight space of the van, and plopped down next to a smiling Ruby.

"I'm so excited," she said. Another snort. "I don't have to keep talking to the back of your head."

I would have been excited too if what I saw next hadn't terrified me.

They pulled the still kicking girl lengthwise onto the bench seat, lying down on her back with long, velcro straps holding her tight. Travis was the last to climb down out of the van, but before he did, he leaned in close over the girl's screaming face.

"Be a good girl," he said in a calm voice, "or I'll have to kill you—put a plastic bag over your head and toss you into a deep ravine. Good girls live. Bad girls die."

The screaming voice went quiet. Travis cocked his head in my direction, and one corner of his mouth curled into a repulsive grin. Another wink.

I waited until we were back on the highway, climbing up into the Rocky Mountains with the radio playing Southern Man by Neil Young, before leaning toward Ruby and whispering, "Do you think he meant it?"

"No," she whispered back. "It's probably just something he says to scare them."

But I could tell from the wrinkles on Ruby's freckled forehead she was scared too.

We rode for hours without speaking, Travis behind the wheel again. The only sounds were the road and the old classic rock hits that played on the radio. I watched aspens and pine trees, and the dark silhouettes of mountain peaks pass by outside the window until my eyes grew heavy. Still, sleep wouldn't come easily.

Good girls live. Bad girls die. Why had Travis said that? And why did he look at me right after he said it?

It was only when Ruby's head lolled over onto my shoulder that I rested my head against the top of hers and drifted off to sleep.

Another gas station, this time along an empty stretch of highway in Utah. We were shuffled back and forth under flickering overhead lights to the dingy bathroom. The night air tingled my skin, and a soft breeze carried the scent of cattle somewhere off in the dark.

Another round of paper bags and tiny water bottles were passed around. Another bruised apple and uninspiring sandwich.

"What do you want to do with her?" Monica motioned over her shoulder to the now-quiet girl, still strapped to the bench seat. "You think she'll give us a hard time?"

"Fuck her," said Travis. "It's four hours to St. George, and then she's not our problem anymore."

"But what if she has to pee?"

"Let her piss her pants. That's what she gets for being a bad girl."

Monica sighed and shrugged her shoulders before climbing into the driver's seat for her turn behind the wheel. In another minute, the van pulled back onto the open highway.

"Wait," said the girl, who was still wearing the spit hood over her head. Her voice cracked and strained, tired from her earlier screams. "I'll be good. I promise. Just let me go to the bathroom."

"Too late," said Travis. "Should have thought of that before you spit on me."

From my place next to Ruby, I heard the girl whimper and what sounded like they might be tears. In another life, I would have demanded they stop the van. I would have stood up for what I believed was right. But out here in the middle of nowhere, I was somebody different. My hands and legs were chained, and I was becoming more and more afraid of the man who held the keys.

It was Denise who spoke up from the back seat. "She's still a person. Let the girl use the bathroom."

"Quiet," he said.

Monica turned up the radio.

But Denise wasn't giving up. "It ain't right, Travis, and you know it. Come on, Monica, you gonna get let him get away with this?"

"Shut your mouth, Denise." His voice shook with unsteady anger. "Or I'll shut it for you."

Denise muttered under her breath. "Bastard."

Travis didn't seem to hear her because he turned back around and went to work on his sandwich. I wondered if all the long hours on the road were getting to him or if something much more sinister lurked beneath the surface.

It had been the same with Matt, the anger slowly bubbling up in little fits and bursts until it finally boiled over. I twisted my wrists in the tight handcuffs, felt the shackles still squeezing my ankles. I wanted to run. Run like I'd done so many times before. But there was no running now. I was a prisoner. His prisoner. And I was totally helpless.

An hour passed. More classic rock hits on the radio. We sat without talking, the only other sound the soft crunching of apples in the dark.

A big sign flashed in the headlights: DO YOU HAVE GAS? NO SERVICES FOR 115 MILES.

Another whimper, and the gentle trickle of liquid splashing onto the floor.

I looked down and saw the puddle of urine, the motion of the van inching it slowly toward my feet.

SEVEN

The sky was clear. Its rich blue color and a single puffy cloud reflected on the glassy waters of the lake. I hung my legs over the long dock and dipped a toe in, sending tiny, gentle ripples out in perfect circles.

The water was cool. Refreshing. Renewing. And as I swam out beyond the dock, it was as if my time in the van had only been a distant nightmare, fading until it would soon be forgotten.

Something tickled my foot. I imagined it was only a gentle fish. But soon, it wrapped itself around my ankle and tightened its grip.

I struggled to break free, and with each kick and pull of my leg, whatever was holding me grew tighter and tighter until it began pulling me beneath the surface.

I couldn't breathe. My mouth filled with water. I struggled to break the surface one last time and screamed for someone, anyone to help me. But I knew in that place I was alone. No help would come.

I closed my eyes and let the water take me. Down. Down. Down ever deeper into that bottomless lake, until there was nothing but darkness.

"Spencer."

Someone called my name, and when I opened my eyes, I found myself still in the van.

"Are you okay?" It was Ruby, soft, and gentle.

Okay? No, I'm not okay.

"I'm fine," I said. "Just a nightmare. How long have I been asleep?"

"I don't know." She leaned over just enough to place a delicate kiss on my cheek. "Try to go back to sleep. I won't let anything happen to you."

But it was Ruby who fell asleep first, head rolling onto my shoulder again. I watched the miles disappear under the headlights of the van and listened to her quiet breath.

We'd been heading west on I-70 ever since leaving Topeka, that much I knew from the road signs. Now we came to an interchange, where I-70 ends and I-15 heads north, to Salt Lake City, and southwest, all the way to Los Angeles. I wondered if I closed my eyes, I might dream this time of palm trees and waves crashing on the beach.

Monica eased the van around a wide turn and merged into the southbound lanes. The only other vehicles on the road were big rigs pulling trailers, drivers paid by the mile racing through the night to deliver their loads.

I did sleep again, but there were no palm trees, only the empty sleep that comes from complete exhaustion.

We arrived at St. George, Utah, as the first sliver of sunlight broke over the horizon, bathing everything in a warm, red glow. The night before, as we'd climbed up and over the Rocky Mountains, there had been pine and aspen forests beyond the window. St. George stood in stark contrast, with its cacti and manicured, bright green golf courses set against the desert scenery.

Monica backed the van into yet another secure garage behind a sign that read: Purgatory Correctional Facility.

There was more of what by now had become a familiar routine, our own sort of purgatory: Shuffling off to the bathroom, munching on dry cheese sandwiches in brown paper bags while Travis and Monica went through the formalities of loading and unloading prisoners.

The young girl who'd spent the night wet with her own piss put up no fight as she was escorted, on wobbly legs, from the van. No one bothered cleaning up the mess.

Travis took his turn at the wheel, and we were off again, a straight shot to Las Vegas, as the cool morning gave way to the hot afternoon sun that poured through the window and baked my skin.

This time it was Denise's turn. She was pulled from the backseat with little ceremony, turning only at the last moment to speak over her shoulder before being shuffled away. "Don't let them grind you down."

When it was over, and we were packed back up in the van, Monica slapped her hands together with a kind of gleeful satisfaction. "Sin City. Home sweet home. It's been quite the run, Travis. But this girl could really use a stiff drink and a good night's sleep in my own bed."

"Well, shoot, Monica. Your replacement ain't even here yet, and already you're trying to scramble away from me. Do I smell that bad?"

She sniffed her own armpit and laughed. I think it was the first time I'd seen her laugh during the whole trip from Kansas. "After three days in the van, we all start to get a bit smelly."

The phone in the center console rang—the same phone that had rung when we'd made our unexpected stop for burgers and milkshakes. Travis answered and nodded along to what I imagined might be some higher up in a cushy corporate office somewhere.

"Bad news," he said, hanging up the phone. "Your replacement called in sick. Corporate wants you to stay on until the next pickup in Salt Lake."

Monica slammed a hand down on the dashboard. "Oh, come on! Don't they know I haven't been home for two weeks? Before this run, they had me crashed out in some dumpy motel in Little Rock. I want my bed. I want my family."

"One more day," he said. "They promised to get you some relief in Salt Lake and a flight back to Vegas tomorrow morning. It's overtime, you know. I'm sure you could use the extra money, what with your brother being sick and all."

"Fine. Let's go then. The sooner we get to Salt Lake, the better."

"That's the spirit." He dropped the van into reverse, and soon we were back on the highway, miles and miles of empty desert dotted only by the occasional cluster of tiny houses or mobile homes passing by outside the window.

I found myself glad Monica would be with us for one more day. I could hardly describe her as an uplifting presence, but she was professional, a check on Travis' more impulsive urges. At least Salt Lake was closer to Portland than Vegas. I'd been in shackles for almost two days and wondered if I would ever be able to walk straight again. Maybe this was my life now, jumpsuits and bars and chains between my ankles. I tried to focus on what Denise had said, but remembering what she looked like as they shuffled her away only reminded me of what I must have looked like to anyone staring back at me—the girl in the pink scrubs.

My depressing thoughts were interrupted by Travis, who was smiling at me in the rear-view mirror. "Don't you worry now, girls. Monica might be leaving us in Salt Lake, but you've got me all the way to the bitter end."

Lucky us.

I hoped by "bitter end," he meant the Multnomah County Jail. I should have known from the hungry sparkle in his eyes that Travis had other plans.

EIGHT

The road trip is a cultural institution as American as baseball and apple pie. Time is different out on the road. The scenery is always changing, reminding you of what a great big space we all live in. But no matter how far you go, how many miles disappear behind you with the meandering perception of time, you're still in the same place—just a tiny dot moving across a map, dragging the weight of your past and your own thoughts along with you.

"Don't you ever wonder about all those people?" Ruby's voice was a welcome relief. Somehow she always knew when to speak, a life preserver in the sea of my darkest thoughts.

"What people?"

"It looks empty, doesn't it? The countryside? But look closely, and you'll see old white houses ringed with peeling picket fences—farms and barns and rows of crops planted by a pair of calloused hands. Sometimes even a few dozen houses clustered together around a Dairy Queen and a steepled church. Every one of them has a story. Life and death. Happiness and sadness. The same story told over and over, each time in a different way."

Just then, I caught sight of an old rusty tractor, sitting alone and long-abandoned to the elements in the middle of an empty field.

"You ever wonder about those people? Where they came from? Where they're going?"

"I don't know, Ruby." It was true. I'd never given much thought to anyone outside of my life in Portland. Maybe I was selfish, or maybe life had just been too hard to think about the world beyond myself.

"When I was a little girl, my grandparents had a farm."

"Oh, yeah?"

"Well, it wasn't much of a farm really—just a few acres of rocky soil and a muddy pond with no fish. Anyway, one spring, my older brother and I each got a piglet to raise from the local 4H club. You should have seen them, Spencer. Such cute little things, tiny squeals as they fed from the bottle. I raised mine like a baby, even won a ribbon at the county fair."

"That's a nice story, Ruby."

"But I'm not finished yet. You see, by winter, mine was the fatter of the two, and Grandpa decided it would make a nice Christmas dinner."

"He killed it?"

"Oh, no. He said I'd raised a life, and it was time I learned what it meant to take one. Of course, I cried and cried and begged him not to make me do it. But when Christmas day finally came, he pinned my sweet little pig down on the cold, snowy ground as my trembling hand slit its squealing throat."

It was hard to picture the soft-spoken, nerdy girl on the seat beside taking a knife to an animal's throat.

A single tear rolled down her cheek. "When it was over, and the blood had been washed from my still-trembling hands, Grandpa sat me down on his lap in the living room while Grandma got to work in the kitchen. And you know what? I'll never forget what he said to me that day."

"What?"

"He said that sadness isn't the hard part of life. Sadness comes easily. He said the hard part, and the only thing in this life really worth doing, is finding a way to be happy with all that sadness around you."

"Your grandfather sounds like a wise man, but I still think he shouldn't have made you kill the pig."

Ruby's mouth curled into a little smile. "Yeah, maybe not. But Spencer, try to find a way to be happy, even with so much madness in the world."

"Okay," I said, not knowing whether or not I was telling her the truth. "I'll try."

"Promise?"

"Yeah, I promise."

I read somewhere once that prisoners in solitary confinement sleep sixteen or more hours a day. I don't know if it's true, but I can't imagine there's much else to do when you spend twenty-three hours a day locked in a concrete cage.

The van had become our cage, and like the prisoners in solitary confinement, we didn't have much to do besides sleep away the long hours on the road.

I was endlessly glad they'd left me beside Ruby. I hoped she and I would keep in touch when this was all over and that maybe I'd even visit her someday in Denver liked I'd promised. Maybe I'd even keep my promise about trying to be happy.

We passed the I-70 interchange, the same place we'd turned and headed south to St. George, as the afternoon faded into evening. Only this time, we kept straight north on I-15, in the direction of a big sign that read: SALT LAKE CITY, 176 MILES.

Travis pulled off the highway at a little town called Fillmore and gassed up the van. Monica shuffled us off to the bathroom, and sack lunches were passed around.

Then it was her turn behind the wheel, as we closed the final stretch through the Utah Valley toward the distant glowing lights of the city.

"I'm going to call ahead," she said, reaching for the company-issued phone.

"You're driving." Travis made a clicking sound with his mouth. "Safety first, remember. I'll make the call."

"Fine." She handed him the phone. "Tell 'em to make sure the pickup is ready, and my replacement is waiting."

I watched from the second-row bench seat as he punched some numbers into the phone. Then the screen went dark as if he'd turned it off rather than pressing send.

"It's Vogel and Lujan, just checking in. Oh, I see ... yes, ma'am ... there must be another option ... okay, I'll pass that along. Canceled? So it's straight through to Oregon? Right ... we'll do our best."

"What did they say?" Monica's hands twisted around the steering wheel. It was clear from Travis' somber tone on the phone she was expecting the worst.

"Do you want the bad news first? Or the really bad news?"

"Just tell me, Travis."

"Okay, okay. But don't shoot the messenger. Seems our prisoner pickup in Salt Lake has been canceled."

"And?"

"And the relief driver canceled too."

"God da—" Monica stopped herself and took a deep breath. "They promised me they would have someone waiting there. You said it yourself."

"What can I say?" Travis laughed—a nervous little chuckle that barely escaped his lips. "I'm sorry, Monica. You know how bad corporate is."

"No, Travis. I won't do it. You need to call them back."

"They were pretty insistent, even pulled out the old line from the corporate handbook about 'mandatory duties' and 'failure to comply could result in termination.' I wouldn't push it if I were you. I know how badly you need this job."

"What am I gonna my mother, my brother?"

"Look, we gotta straight shot all the way through to Portland. No more pickups or drop-offs until we get there. Corporate said they'll book you on the first flight out back to Vegas."

"Yeah, like I'm supposed to trust them after my last two relief drivers didn't show up?"

It was the second time in two days I'd felt sorry for her. I'd worked enough crappy jobs to know management has little sympathy for front line workers. The only thing they care about is the bottom line.

Travis appeared to be doing his best to console her. He even offered to drive back-to-back shifts through the night so she could get some extra rest. But still, I couldn't help thinking about what I'd seen. Had he really turned off the phone, or had the screen just gone dark at the exact moment he'd placed the call? Why would he fake a call like that? Surely, the GPS on the van would alert the corporate office if we failed to stop in Salt Lake City as planned.

I'd look back on that moment many times in the coming weeks. Had I known then what was going to happen, I would have warned her. I would have screamed and kicked and bit through the chains with cracked teeth. I would have broken every bone in my hands and torn the skin from my fingers to escape the cuffs around my wrists. No price, no pain, would have been too great.

But doubt is a funny thing, and hindsight, as they say, is always 20/20. Like those people who go through life believing nothing bad could ever really happen to them, I told myself that everything would be okay. I couldn't be sure of what I'd seen. Who was I to accuse him of lying to Monica? Or perhaps it was something more that kept me from speaking up—the hint of fear I felt whenever he winked at me or whenever I caught him staring back at me in the rear-view mirror with hunger in his eyes.

Instead, I did the one thing so many of us do when we're faced with uncertainty. Nothing.

Besides, I was still so very tired, and Ruby felt so warm beside me. *It'll be okay. You'll see. It was all just a silly misunderstanding.*

I dreamed of the lake again, of hands pulling me down and down and down into its bottomless abyss.

When I woke, we were alone on a dark stretch of highway, not a single house or light from another vehicle anywhere in sight.

Travis was behind the wheel, humming along quietly to a Steely Dan song on the radio.

And Monica? Monica was gone.

NINE

Where's Monica? It was all I could think about as I sat frozen, my thoughts spinning faster than the wheels on the road as the dark interior of the van closed in around me. It was like the recurring nightmare I'd had as a child, buried alive in a tiny wooden box. Only this wasn't a nightmare. There would be no waking up in my bed.

Breathe. Surely, I imagined, there must have been some explanation. Maybe Monica was just lying down on the bench seat behind me, catching up on some must needed sleep. I wanted to twist around, peer over my shoulder, and confirm my desperate hope that we weren't really alone on some desolate road in the middle of nowhere with Travis. But if I moved, he'd know I was awake.

Too late. Our eyes met in the rear-view mirror, his face glowing a dull green from the lights on the dashboard.

"Shhh," he said, bringing a finger up to his lips. "Don't want to wake Ruby. It's been a long day for everyone. Go back to sleep."

I was surprised when I found myself wanting to do exactly what he'd said. Maybe if I closed my eyes and went back to sleep, it would be morning when I woke, and there'd be some perfectly good explanation for what had happened as we slept.

Maybe it was hope, or denial, like when people tell themselves the plane they're on could never crash. Oh no, they say, that could never happen to me. Until it does.

"Where is she, Travis?"

Ruby stirred beside me, her tiny body shifting around in place beneath the chains.

"Look," he said, "I didn't want to worry you. I'll explain everything when we stop for breakfast in the morning."

Ruby yawned. "What's the matter? What's happening?"

"It's Monica," I said. "She's gone."

"What do you mean she's gone?"

"I don't know, and Travis won't tell me where she is."

"Now hold on," he said. "I'm not in the business of keeping secrets. Monica quit."

"Quit?"

"Yep, about a hundred miles outside of Salt Lake. One minute she was talking about how much she missed her family, and the next minute she was telling me to stop the van at some one-horse town alongside the road. Said something about hitching a ride back to the city, and then she just walked away."

You expect me to believe that?

"It's this job," he said. "It gets to you after a while, all the miles zigzagging back and forth, the lack of sleep. Hell, I've thought about quitting myself. I guess she just—snapped."

I knew Monica had been under a lot of pressure. She had a sick brother back home, and her corporate overlords weren't doing her any favors. But still, it seemed unlike her to quit so suddenly.

"I hope she's okay," said Ruby. "You shouldn't have let her go."

Travis raised his hands off the wheel and shrugged his shoulders. "Hey, it's a free country. It's not like I could have done anything to stop her."

Kind of an ironic thing to say to two girls in matching sets of shackles.

"But don't you worry." He drummed his fingers on the dashboard. "I've already called it in. Not much we can do now but keep going. Got a new pickup in Boise, and another female guard will meet us there, ride with us the rest of the way into Portland."

I thought about what he'd said. It kind of made sense. Everything except for the part about Monica walking away in the dead of night. I found some comfort when I remembered the van had a GPS tracker, and any deviation from our route would alert the corporate office. Besides, what could I do? I was a prisoner, his prisoner. The only thing I had to cling to was some small hope that what he'd said was true.

Ruby leaned toward me and rested her head on my shoulder. "It'll be okay," she whispered. "You'll see."

I spent the night wide awake, replaying his story over and over again in my head, trying to find something that would put my mind at ease. Minutes stretched into long hours until finally, the first hint of dawn fought back the night sky. Everything would feel better, safer, in the bright light of day.

But something wasn't right. We were driving toward the sun, whose rays had just begun to pour in through the windshield. I'd hardly been a good geography student, but I knew beyond any doubt that Boise and Portland were west of Salt Lake City. That's when it hit me.

East. We're driving east.

I screamed.

Ruby jolted awake and looked at me with wide eyes.

I didn't wait for her to ask me what was wrong. "He lied," I said, hands jerking against the cuffs and the chain secured tightly around my waist. "Travis lied. We're not going to Boise. We're driving east."

Her still-wide eyes shifted forward, anticipating some kind of response from the man behind the wheel.

"Did I say Boise?" He looked back at us in the rear-view mirror. "I meant Idaho Falls. Guess I've been on the road for too long. All these towns start to become the same."

"Stop the van." My breath quickened. The all-too-familiar feeling of claustrophobia gripped my chest, and I fought harder against the chains.

"No can do," he said. "You know the drill. All stops must be approved in advance."

"Please, I can't breathe." Two invisible hands had wrapped themselves around my throat. Even the seatbelt had become an unbearable weight, holding me down with some unimaginable pressure.

"Relax. Everything's fine. We'll stop for breakfast soon, and you'll feel better."

"Please," said Ruby. "She needs help. I think she's having a panic attack."

She turned back to me and tried to soothe me with a calm voice. "Count to ten. That's it. Just breathe, Spencer. You can do it. Just breathe."

But it was all too much. The long days crammed in the back of the van. The shackles. The chains. And the striking realization that I really was as helpless as I'd suspected, despite my best efforts to deny the truth of my worsening situation.

Then the world spun, and everything went black.

I couldn't say whether I'd been out for hours or only a few minutes, but when I opened my eyes, the van was stopped in the parking lot of a roadside rest stop. The double doors had been opened wide, and a fresh breeze cooled my clammy skin.

Travis came around from the back and unlocked one side of my handcuffs before passing me a water bottle. "Splash a little on your face. It'll help."

"Thanks."

"Look," he said. "I'm sorry. It's all my fault. If I hadn't mixed up the towns, none of this would have happened."

I didn't want to forgive him. His apology seemed genuine, but there was still something about him I didn't trust. I took a long sip from the bottle and tried to think of something to say.

He spoke again first. "We've got another scheduled stop in about an hour. If you can hold tight until then, we'll get you out of the van and stretch your legs for a few minutes. I know it's a long ride, all this crisscrossing around, but after Idaho Falls, we're headed straight to Portland."

I took another sip and nodded.

"That's my girl," he said as he fastened the handcuff back around my wrist.

That's my girl?

I wasn't anyone's girl. Maybe that's what had always bothered Matt. He wanted to think of me as just another possession, like that stupid car he'd brag about to friends.

Instead, I'd always been independent. A partner? Sure. But a possession, something to dress up and drag along to fancy company dinners to make the other guys in the office drool? Not my style.

At least Travis was back to being friendly. Another stop would do us some good, and I'd find out soon enough if he was really telling the truth about Idaho Falls. I didn't want to think about what might happen if he wasn't.

Ruby smiled. "Feeling better?"

"Yes, a little."

"You had me pretty worried about you."

"I'll be okay." In truth, I still wasn't so sure. But I didn't see much use in sharing my lingering concerns with her.

"Have you ever had a panic attack before?"

"Yes, but not since the years after my mom died."

Her smiled curl down into a frown. "Maybe you should talk to somebody about that. I mean, I know it sounds a bit silly. But believe me, it really helps."

I tried imagining Ruby, quirky but resilient Ruby, spread on some therapist's couch. "Yeah, maybe. I've been seeing one here and there. But between you and me, I've spent most of the years since my mom died just trying to survive on my own."

I could see the love and compassion in her eyes. "You'll be alright, Spencer. Don't ask me how I know. I just know."

"You're a true friend, Ruby. Maybe the best friend I've ever had."

It might not be easy for me to tell you this, but I love you.

TEN

As promised, Travis pulled the van into a roadside truck stop with a big rotating sign in the shape of a donut. The road had narrowed down to two lanes, and low mountains rose up on all sides.

"This is gonna be hard," he said, "on account of Monica not being here. I'm sure you girls won't be any trouble. Help me out, and I'll buy us all a box of donuts."

"I have to pee real bad," said Ruby. "Is it alright if I go first?"

Travis leaned in over me to unbuckle her seat belt, and I could smell the coffee on his breath. Then it was Ruby's turn to shuffle around me, snorting and saying she was sorry as she bumped my knees.

When Ruby was out beside the van, Travis produced a long chain and locked it securely to the links in the center of her handcuffs. "I hate to do this," he said. "But I've got to use a lead chain since I'm not inclined to follow you into the bathroom."

I watched through the mesh cage over the window as they went off towards the restaurant and the bathrooms, Ruby shuffling along in front of Travis as he held the other end of the chain.

Minutes passed. Travis had taken the keys along with him, and the van, devoid of any air-conditioning or ventilation, began to warm up in the mid-morning sun.

It's the moments when you have nothing to do but wait, that your mind starts to wander. And as I sat in the back of that stuffy van, I relived everything that had happened over the last few days. The creepy winks and smiles. The milkshake and the brush against my knee. Monica's mysterious disappearance in the middle of the night. And the words Travis had whispered to the poor girl strapped to the bench seat as he looked me in the eyes: *Good girls live. Bad girls die.*

I wondered then if I might be able to escape. Maybe when it was my turn to go to the bathroom, I could find some way out the back. Maybe I could choke him with the chain, grab the keys to the van, and make a break for it with Ruby. He'd have the handcuff keys too. If I could get the shackles off, maybe we'd have a chance. Where we went from there didn't matter. I only wanted to get us as far away from him as possible, even if that meant turning ourselves in at some police station a hundred or so miles down the road.

Am I crazy? It was certainly a crazy idea. The sensible thing would have been to wait and see if Monica's replacement was actually waiting for us in Idaho Falls. But what if it was all just a big lie? Maybe then it would be too late to do anything about it. Maybe by then, we'd both be dead. No, I had to take the chance. Something deep inside, some feeling down in my gut, told me it was the only chance I was going to get.

I worked it all out in my head. I'd play along nicely and wait until we were headed back to the van. Then I'd stumble, pretending to trip over the shackles. When he bent over to help me up, I'd make my move.

I was so lost in thought I didn't see them come back to the van. I jumped when the door opened.

"You okay?" Ruby held a box of donuts between her cuffed hands.

"Yeah, I'm fine. It's getting pretty hot back here. I think I dozed off for a minute."

Travis unlocked the chain and helped her back into the seat, reached across my lap again to fasten her seatbelt, and then unfastened mine. "I'll put the A/C on when we get back on the road."

Then it was my turn to climb out. I took a moment to steady myself as Travis locked the long chain to the handcuffs around my wrists. Then we shuffled off together toward the restaurant, Travis guiding me like some master walking a human dog on a leash.

A tiny bell above the door dinged.

"Back again?" said an enormous woman behind a long counter. Local news flickered and flashed on a TV in one corner, but the woman's attention was focused on a gossip magazine. She'd hardly bothered to look up as we entered.

By now, I'd become accustomed to the stares and ignored the whispers exchanged between the few patrons, mostly old truckers, spread out on stools in front of the counter or milling about the aisles stuffed with junk food and pornographic magazines.

"This way," said Travis, pointing to a swinging door that led to a long, back hallway.

When we got to the lady's room, he unlocked one of my cuffs and told me to go inside. My hands fumbled nervously as I dropped the pink pants down around my ankles, Travis still holding the long length of chain outside the door.

You can do this. Just breathe, Spencer. Breathe.

I glanced at myself in the bathroom mirror on the way out and was shocked at my own appearance. Who was this girl, who only weeks before, had been sipping cocktails with her friends in a trendy Portland bar? Now she was somewhere in Idaho, no makeup on her face, bags underneath her eyes, with her hands chained to her waist.

This, too, shall pass. Someday, this will all be behind you.

The chain between my ankles clinked as we shuffled back out along the counter. We'd almost made it to the door when something on the TV caught my attention. It was the outline of a body in some muddy ditch, a white sheet draped over the top. Beneath the image, bold letters flashed across the screen: FEMALE PRISON GUARD FOUND DEAD IN A ROADSIDE DITCH. OFFICIALS IN UTAH BELIEVE TWO FEMALE PRISONERS ARE THE SUSPECTS. THE WHEREABOUTS OF ONE ADDITIONAL GUARD ARE STILL UNKNOWN.

My heart leaped into my throat. My worst suspicions were true, even the ones I'd never allowed to become fully formed thoughts in my head. Travis had murdered Monica as we slept and was taking us somewhere to rape us or torture us, or worse.

He must have seen the news too because he took me by the arm with a firm grip and forced me toward the door.

"It's him," I said to the woman behind the counter. "The dead guard—he killed her."

The woman looked up from her magazine and glanced at the television. The news had already moved on to a local story about the fire department raising funds for the county animal shelter.

"Please," I said, digging in my heels and fighting against his grip. "It's him. You have to help us. He killed her, and he's going to kill us too."

"I'm so sorry for the trouble," he said. "These prisoners will try anything to escape."

The woman only shrugged and went back to her magazine. The little bell above the door dinged again on our way out.

This is it. Now or never.

How I'd rip free from his grip and get the chain around his neck with my hands still cuffed, I didn't know. But I knew at that moment, beyond any shred of doubt, that if I didn't succeed in escaping with Ruby, we were both going to end up dead.

My muscles tensed, and I braced for a fight. Just as I was about to wrest free, a police car pulled into the parking lot and came to a stop beside us. A badge on the side of the door read: BEAR LAKE COUNTY SHERIFF. At least I knew where we were, even though I had no real idea where Bear Lake County might be.

An older man in a brown uniform exited the patrol car and adjusted his wide-brimmed hat. "How's it going there? You having some trouble?"

"No trouble," said Travis. "This one's just not making it easy on me. Been causing problems all the way down from Montana."

"You need a hand, son?"

"Thanks, officer. But I don't want to bother you."

"Oh, it's no bother. Say, you headed south then?"

"Yes, sir, all the way to Albuquerque."

I couldn't believe how easily the lies rolled off his disgusting lips.

"You be careful now. Word came over the radio this morning; they found one of your kind dead in a ditch just across the Utah state line. Strangled, they said. If you ask me, the world's really going to shit."

Travis raised an eyebrow. "Is that so?"

"That's us," I screamed. "He killed her! He killed Monica, and he'll kill us too."

"Now I see what you mean," said the old deputy. "She's a real head case, eh? You sure you don't want some help getting her over to your van?"

"Her bark is worse than her bite." Travis laughed. "You stay safe out there, officer."

"I could say the same to you, young man." The deputy raised a gloved hand and tipped his hat. "It's a crazy world—just keeps getting crazier by the day."

I watched the old man disappear into the store, all my hopes for a rescue disappearing with him. Still, I fought Travis all the way back to the van with whatever strength I managed to muster. I fought like my life depended on it because I was convinced it did. But with my hands chained to my waist and my legs in shackles, it wasn't much of a fight.

He swung the van door open with a burst of violence and forced me inside. Ruby screamed too when she saw what was happening. The pink box on her lap fell to the floor, and colorful donuts rolled under the seats.

I kicked with both feet and screamed along with her, landing one good blow to his face before he pinned me down with all of his bodyweight. When the seatbelt was fastened, and the fight had gone out of me, he leaned in close, so close I could smell his putrid breath, and whispered in my ear, "Good girls live. Bad girls die."

ELEVEN

The tires kicked up gravel behind us as the van tore out of the parking lot. I was still struggling against the chains, though tiring quickly. When I looked down, there was blood on my wrists and a blue donut between my feet.

Ruby, whose expression was both shocked and confused, cried as she begged me to tell her what had happened.

"Now look what you made me do," said Travis from behind the steering wheel. "We were all getting along so well. You just had to go and mess it up."

"Please," Ruby said, tears running down her face and falling in darkened spots on her pink shirt. "Please, somebody, tell me what happened."

"He killed her," I said. "It was on the TV, Ruby. They found Monica dead beside the road."

"Oh my god." Ruby's face turned a pale shade of gray, and I thought she might pass out.

"Hold on a minute," he said. "I didn't kill anyone."

"She's dead, Travis. You saw it yourself."

"That doesn't mean I killed her. Look, Ruby was right. I never should have let her walk away like that. Poor Monica probably caught a ride with the wrong person. Things happen all the time out here on these empty roads."

I knew it was insane, but I found myself wishing for a split second what he'd said was true. I was looking for something, anything that might give me some hope we'd make it out of this alive.

And the van! The van has GPS. Someone still knows where we are.

There was only one problem with his story. "If that's true, then why'd you lie to the sheriff's deputy?"

"Look, I was shocked, same as you, when I saw that Monica was found dead. I guess I panicked. I thought maybe they'd blame me, just like you're doing now."

"That a lie. He's lying, Ruby."

"Wait a minute. It ain't nice to call people liars. This is all just a misunderstanding."

"Call it in," I said.

"What?"

"You know, pick up the phone and call the corporate office. Let them know what's going on. If you do that, I'll believe you about everything."

"You're a prisoner, Spencer. You're hardly in a position to be making demands."

"Do it. Put it on speakerphone so we can all hear what they have to say."

"I can't do that," he said.

"Why not?"

"Well, your dear old friend Monica, in her hurry to walk away from the job, took off with the duty phone."

Oh, he's good.

He was so good I was almost ready to believe him. But as the road wound further up into the mountains, we passed a big sign, clear as day: WELCOME TO WYOMING. FOREVER WEST.

Ruby saw it too. "We're not going to Idaho Falls, are we?"

"No," he said in a flat voice. "You got me, okay? We're not going to Idaho Falls."

Ruby screamed again, and I did too.

His gaze met mine in the rear-view mirror, a sparkle in his eyes I'd never seen before as if the truth had somehow set him free.

"I'm doing you a favor," he said. "You really want me to take you back to stand trial? You'd end up in prison. Where I'm taking you will be so much better. Believe me, nobody will ever find you there, and that's the truth."

I thought I might vomit, but instead, I gathered myself up and twisted sideways, chain digging into my stomach until I finally managed to undo my seatbelt.

"Don't do it, Spencer."

But it was too late. I didn't care what he said. He was crazy, and nothing he could say or do would change my mind. "Fuck you," I said, working onto my back and kicking at the wire cage on the window with both feet.

"Please, don't make me stop the van."

But I wasn't listening. I kicked and kicked until the wires bent and the window shattered.

I'd rather throw myself onto the road, hope that some trucker comes along to offer me help than spend another minute in the van with that psycho.

Ruby was still crying in the seat behind me. "Please, Spencer. He seems really mad."

Travis beat his hands against the steering wheel as he pulled the van over and brought it to a stop alongside the two-lane mountain road. "I told you, I'm only trying to help. But you won't listen, so now I gotta stop being the nice guy." He climbed down from the driver's seat and went to the back of the van, then came around to the side and swung open the door. "It's your fault," he said. "Don't forget, it's you who made me do this."

I pivoted on the bench seat with some previously unknown strength and kicked at his face. Another blow found its target, and blood ran from his nose.

Now I saw it—the rage in his eyes. He climbed on top of me and pinned me beneath his bodyweight again. I closed my eyes and screamed until I felt something, a rag or old t-shirt maybe, forced into my mouth and tied tightly around the back of my head. I thought I might die, unable to scream or breathe as the air pumped desperately in and out of my nose. Next came the straps, the same ones they'd used to pin down the girl from Denver. I wondered how long it would be until I pissed myself too.

It was only a few seconds before I felt the adrenaline surging through my veins, the feeling of claustrophobia overwhelming me. Again I thought I might pass out.

But whatever horrors might have come in the days that followed, what I saw next would remain burned in my memory forever. No words could ever describe the look of terror on Ruby's face as he dragged her screaming from the van along that empty stretch of mountain highway. She cried and begged him to stop, the pitiful cries of someone who knew they were about to die and could do nothing to stop it.

I would have screamed too if my mouth wasn't already gagged. Tears welled in my eyes and ran into my nose and threatened to drown me.

The last thing I remember of Ruby was her calling my name, and the moment our eyes made contact as he forced her, kicking and screaming, to an unmarked grave.

It might have been only minutes, but it seemed like an eternity before he returned, blood splattered on his hands and face and neck—Ruby's blood.

How I hated him then. I would have killed him with a rock or my own bare hands had I been able. I would have watched the blood and brains oozing from his cracked skull onto the weather-worn asphalt and laughed as the life drained from his face. It wouldn't be the last time I'd have such fantasies, though my attention quickly turned to the question that burned brightly in my mind.

Is he going to kill me too?

But he didn't lay another finger on me. Instead, he went around back and cleaned up with a bottle of water. I heard the splashing and rubbing from my place still strapped to the bench seat. When he was finished, he closed the double side doors with a delicate touch before climbing into the driver's seat. The engine rumbled to life, and soon we were back on the road, climbing higher into the mountains while

Ruby's body was left to rot in the hot afternoon sun in an otherwise unremarkable ditch somewhere behind us.

Hours passed without a word between us. It wasn't that I didn't want to speak. I wanted to curse him and tell him I'd send him to burn in hell, but the gag stuffed in my mouth prevented me from saying the thoughts that raced through my mind.

Travis did speak, but not to me. He spat and muttered incoherent phrases under his breath as he fidgeted and tapped nervously on the steering wheel.

It was dark when the van finally slowed, and Travis reappeared at the side doors. "I'm going to take the gag out of your mouth, but only if you promise not to scream."

I nodded.

He traced the back of his fingers lightly against my cheek before untying the knot behind my head and slipping the gag out.

"Bastard," I said. "You killed her. You killed Ruby just like you killed Monica."

"Yes," he said, releasing a long sigh. "I killed Monica, and I killed Ruby too. But you have to understand, my dear, sweet Spencer. I did it all for you."

"Fuck you."

"That's okay. Maybe you don't understand it now. One day you will. You're mine now, and I won't let them take you away from me. Not now. Not ever."

As dry as my throat had become, I managed to gather enough saliva to spit in his face.

I expected he might hit me, but instead, he licked the runny saliva from his chapped lips, holding it in his mouth as if he savored the taste. I felt bile rise up and burn the back of my throat.

"You taste good," he said. "I could taste you again and again."

I knew what would come next from the smile that flashed across his face. "No," I said.

But it was too late. He held me down with his clammy hands on my shoulders and leaned forward until his lips touched mine.

As if by instinct, I snapped my head back and slammed it forward, bringing my forehead down hard on his nose. Blood gushed from both nostrils and soiled his shirt.

That's when he slapped me. The back of his hand struck my cheek with a sudden pop that left a loud ringing in my ears.

Even he seemed surprised by his reaction. "I didn't want to do that, Spencer. But you made me. Just like you made me kill Ruby."

"And Monica? Did I make you do that too?"

He smiled again, his teeth stained bright red from the blood that had worked its way into his mouth. "It's okay, Spencer. I forgive you. We'll make a nice girl out of you, I promise."

I screamed and spat as he worked the gag back into my mouth. Then I heard the back door open, and he returned a moment later with some kind of cloth bag, maybe a pillowcase, which he placed over my head.

"Relax now. We've got about eight more hours on the road until we get home. It's going to be a long ride if you wanna keep fighting me."

I almost didn't hear the last thing he said. My breath had quickened again, and I gasped for air. The bag over my head closed in around me, and I thought I might die from suffocation.

This is it. This is the moment I die. Alone in the back of a van with a madman behind the wheel.

I must have passed out again because I don't remember anything from the rest of the drive.

The only thing I remember is that when I finally opened my eyes, the van had stopped. Even with the bag over my head, I knew it was nighttime. The only sounds were the chirping of insects, crickets maybe, and the hoot of an owl somewhere off in the distance.

I steadied myself, waiting for whatever would happen next.

"We're home," he said, as he wrapped his hands around my ankles.

I kicked and kicked and felt my feet strike what I thought might have been his face. He released his grip and cried out in agony.

"My nose," he said. "I think you broke my fucking nose."

Then something hard hit me on the head, and for the second time since we'd left Ruby dead in a ditch, the world spun and went dark.

TWELVE

I couldn't say how much time had passed until I woke with an awful pounding in my head. I lifted my hands toward my face, still expected them to be pinned to my waist by a chain, and was surprised when I touched my own cheeks. My fingers climbed upward until I felt soft gauze—a bandage had been wrapped tightly around my head.

Maybe I've been rescued. I'm in the hospital. I never thought I'd say this, but I'd give anything to see a police officer standing over me.

My hopes evaporated when I felt the now-familiar cuffs around my wrists. Only they were different. Not handcuffs. More like something from an old film, thick bands of metal with a protruding bolt on each side.

And the chain. There was still a chain. This, too, was different than the standard police issue. Heavier. It was dark in whatever room I'd been brought to, but I followed the links of the chain until it came to a ring on a wall. Cold to the touch. Concrete.

A fluorescent light flicked on overhead and sent pain shooting through my head. I squinted and struggled to adjust my eyes to the bright light.

"Welcome home." Travis moved until the light was behind him, his shadow falling across the shackles still secured tightly around my ankles.

"Where are we?"

"My house."

"Your house?"

"Well, not exactly. I'm sure the police will turn up at my apartment when they figure out what's really happened. This is more like a cabin, a hunting lodge, where my uncle used to bring me when I was a kid. The old bastard never did leave a proper will, said he didn't trust lawyers, and the like. But it's mine to use, with no paperwork linking it to my name. Maybe Uncle Bart was right about the lawyers."

"Travis, you have to stop this." My head still throbbed as I struggled to find the right words. "Let me go now, and I won't say anything, I promise. Whatever happened out there with Monica and Ruby will all be forgotten. Just give me back my clothes and drop me alongside the road. I'll hitch a ride from there."

"Now, you and I both know it's never that simple. Besides, I think you're really going to like it here once you learn to behave and start acting like a good girl." He touched the clean white bandage taped across his nose. "I'm afraid we didn't start off on the right foot."

"Look, I'm sorry about that. Real sorry. It was all just a misunderstanding. You're a nice guy, Travis. I know deep down you're a nice guy. But you have to let me go."

"Go where? Back to jail and then on to prison? You're a wanted fugitive. For all the police know, we did it together, killing Monica and Ruby. Or maybe you did it alone and forced me to go along. I bet they think you're headed to Canada right now, or maybe you turned around and headed down south to Mexico."

"Wait a minute—"

"Could be true," he said. "Stranger things have been known to happen."

The very suggestion that I'd had something to do with Ruby's death set my blood boiling. In the back of the van, I'd felt fear—fear for my life. Now all I felt was anger.

"But the van. The van has GPS, Travis. I bet the state troopers are on their way now. It's going to be a lot better if you let me go. I'll tell them you never hurt me."

"GPS?" He laughed. "Come on, Spencer. You really think I'm that stupid? I tore that thing off the undercarriage the night I killed Monica. Tossed it outside the window somewhere just over the Idaho border. And I got news for you, we ain't in Idaho anymore."

He's smarter than I thought.

"Okay, then. So what's your plan?"

"My plan?"

"Yeah, I mean, you can't just keep me chained up in here forever."

"I'll keep you chained up for as long as it takes."

"As long as what takes?"

"Until you love me."

I spit at his feet. "I'll never love you, Travis. You killed Ruby. You killed my friend."

He cocked his head to the side, and one corner of his mouth turned upward into a devilish grin. In the flickering glow of the fluorescent lightbulb, he looked like the sinister psychopath from some horror movie.

That's what he is. A murderer. A psychopath. I'm alone with a psychopath.

I wanted to scream. But so far, screams had done little to save me. I held out some kind of hope that I could talk my way out of this, even if I doubted that would happen.

"Love you?" I said. "Do you think I'd really love someone who keeps me in chains?"

"You will. I know it, Spencer. You're the one."

"Then let's leave together. You said it yourself, we could go to Mexico. Take long walks on the beach and drink cocktails with little paper umbrellas."

His gaze softened as if he were staring off into the distance, imaging the possibility. "That would be nice. But we're not there yet. You don't love me. I have to know you love me first."

Maybe I should just say I love him.

The idea made me sick, and I thought I tasted bile again in the back of my throat. "So what are you going to do, just leave me here? Where am I going to pee?"

He pointed. "There's a bucket over there in the corner. I'll bring you some food in the morning."

"A bucket?"

"Don't worry. I'll empty it twice a day."

Wow. So chivalrous. It's like he thinks he's actually doing me some kind of favor.

"You should rest now."

"Wait—"

He reached for a switch on the wall, and the room went dark. I listened for footsteps but heard only the slightest whistle as he breathed in and out of his broken nose. I imagined him standing there in the black, empty space of the room, hovering over me like some kind of ghost.

"Spencer?" he said.

I didn't answer.

"I love you. You'll see. I love you."

And then he was gone.

THIRTEEN

I stayed awake for a long time, too terrified to close my eyes and too bothered by the pounding pain in my head.

Some situation you've found yourself in, Spencer.

It was like one of those cheap thriller novels my first roommate, Sarah, used to read when she was too stoned to bother putting on clothes or leaving the apartment—the ones where the wife murders the husband and frames his mistress or the serial killer stalks the female police detective assigned to hunt him down.

Only this wasn't a cheap thriller. It was my life. Looking back on that first night in Travis's cabin, I should have been more terrified than I was. But it's hard to grasp the reality of the situation in the moment, however terrible it might be.

I closed my eyes and rested my head against the concrete wall.

Somewhere outside, I heard an owl hooting and wondered if it was the same one I'd heard before Travis had knocked me over the head. In the days and weeks to come, I would long to be that owl—spread my wings and fly off into the night, my feathers silhouetted against a full moon. Only I wasn't an owl. There would be no flying away.

I've often wondered how people manage to sleep in impossible circumstances. Soldiers in a cold, wet trench, bullets whizzing over their heads. Migrants crossing the Mediterranean Sea in a rubber raft, sharks circling in the blue waters all around them.

But the body wants what it wants. So it was some late hour deep in the night that I finally curled up on the musty, damp floor and drifted off to sleep.

The heavenly scent of eggs and bacon frying in a hot pan filled the air. A ray of sunlight poured in through a tiny window high in the wall. It was almost as if I'd woken up in a different place, just another weekend trip to the cabin with my high school friend Felicity.

I closed my eyes and tried to imagine it was true. Travis' heavy footsteps on the wooden stairs were quick to destroy my thinly-conceived fantasy.

"Good morning," he said. He was no longer in his company-issued uniform. Instead, he wore a red flannel shirt and a pair of jeans. Standing there with the plate of bacon and eggs in his hand, he looked almost like a hipster waiter at a Portland all-night diner. "I thought you might want some real food after all those cheese sandwiches."

He put the plate down on the concrete floor, an arm's length from me, and pulled an old wooden chair from the opposite corner of the room.

The hunger in my stomach threatened to send me leaping for the plate, scooping long strips of greasy bacon into my mouth like some kind of wild animal. But I didn't want to give him the satisfaction of feeling good about himself. I didn't want to be the animal in his zoo.

"It's okay," he said. "Maybe you're not hungry."

I thought he might take the plate away, but he left it sitting in front of me.

"Eat whenever you like. Maybe someday soon, we could enjoy our meals together."

Why, yes, honey! That would be great—you pouring me another glass of champagne and passing the oysters across the table as I sit chained to the wall, a bucket of my own shit fermenting in the corner.

"Yes," I said. "That would be nice."

If only for the opportunity to stab you with a fork.

He raised an eyebrow. "Don't lie, Spencer. Only bad girls lie. You're not ready yet, but that will change when you see how much I love you."

"If you really love me, why don't you prove it?"

"How?"

"You can start by jumping off a bridge."

He laughed. "You see, that's why I like you. You've got a little fire in your belly. I knew from the moment I laid eyes on you in Topeka, you'd be a challenge. But anything worth doing takes work, right? You're not like that stupid—"

"Like what? Like who?"

"Nothing," he said. "I'm gonna make a supply run, go into town and get stocked up on everything we need to stay out here for a while. Enjoy your breakfast."

I watched him climb back up the stairs. He was young and in good shape, but today he seemed even lighter on his feet than he had during the long days in the van.

He's excited. He's happy. He actually thinks something good might come from this.

I waited until I heard a vehicle's engine roar to life and the crunching of tires on a gravel driveway. As the sound slowly moved away and disappeared, I inched forward and lifted the plate.

Could the eggs be poisoned?

No, that didn't make sense. Why would he go through all the trouble of kidnapping me just to poison me with eggs? I lifted a strip of bacon to my nose and sniffed. It was smoky—real bacon, not like that fake, vegan stuff they serve in half the restaurants in Portland.

I wanted to put the plate back down just to spite him, to see the disappointed look on his face when he came back to find the plate exactly where he'd left it. But I was too hungry. I brought the bacon to my lips and took a small bite. Chewed. Swallowed. Delicious.

When the bacon was gone, I moved on to the eggs. He'd left me without a fork, so I scooped the eggs into my mouth with a piece of buttered toast. I'd never been so happy for such a simple meal. Even on the streets, after I'd found myself eighteen and no longer in foster care, there had been homeless shelters and soup kitchens—friends who'd fed me and let me crash on sofas. And the punk house with my first boyfriend, Derek, who played in a shitty band and wore the same smelly, leather jacket for years after it should have been tossed in a dumpster.

There was another memory too. Matt bringing me eggs in bed and telling me he loved me. He'd kiss me on the forehead before leaving for work, and when he'd come home late in the evening, he'd take me out for a romantic dinner at my favorite Thai restaurant.

Matt never needed the chains. He'd done what so many men do, swept me off my feet with compliments and adoration, always playing the perfect gentleman. It was only later when he knew I'd come to rely on his support, that he'd threaten to withhold his love as a means to control me.

Little by little, he seized power. First, it was the cell phone he'd added to his plan so he could monitor the record of my calls. Then it was the joint bank account. No need for my own anymore, he'd said. Besides, it wasn't like I ever had any real money in there anyway.

Like a frog in a pot of water, by the time I realized what was happening, it was too late. Until the night I came home to find him pacing back and forth, and everything fell apart.

Travis was a more obvious danger. Unlike Matt, who'd only threatened to kill me, Travis was a confirmed killer. As I swallowed the last of the eggs and toast and licked the plate clean, I wondered if Monica and Ruby were the only ones. Perhaps there were others left to rot on the side of some empty road. More bodies tossed into ravines.

I returned the plate to the place where he'd left it and surveyed the room. The walls and floor were all concrete, with wooden beams holding up the ceiling above. A single high window, my only source of light, might have been too small to crawl through. And it didn't matter. A metal grid of welded rebars had been bolted over the opening.

In one corner was the wooden chair Travis had taken a seat on, and in the opposite corner sat an old washer and a dryer, their pea-green exteriors chipped and faded.

I found a bottle of water set neatly beside the bucket and drank. The cool liquid soothed my throat, which had gone raw from the previous day's screaming. Food and water. A bucket for my business. It was all one needed to live when you subtract love and sunshine and the company of friends.

I guessed we were somewhere far from the city. He'd said it was an old hunting cabin, which meant it would likely be set back some distance from any kind of well-trafficked road. Even if I managed to escape, I would face a long hike over unknown terrain. It was a chance I might have to take.

Better to die lost in the forest or the mountains than in his basement dungeon.

But there was the problem of the chains running from each of my wrists to a heavy ring bolted deep into the concrete wall. And the shackles, the same ones I'd worn since leaving the jail in Topeka, still dug into the skin around my ankles.

Escape seemed like an impossibility.

Don't cry. Not here. Not like this.

Crying meant giving up, letting him win. I had to be strong, even if it meant eating his food. Even if it meant shitting and pissing into a plastic bucket.

Crap. Now I have to pee.

I'd grown accustomed to squatting in shackles during the many stops we'd made on the road. As I braced myself against the wall and listened to the splashing of piss in the bottom of the bucket, I distracted myself with thoughts of rescue.

I imagined the police bursting into the cabin and the pathetic sound of Travis whimpering as they carried him away. Maybe he'd put up a fight, and they'd shoot him. That would be even better.

Sure, he'd tossed out the GPS device, but sooner or later, the police would put things together and figure out it was him. Maybe they'd find Ruby's body. I hoped they'd find Ruby's body. The thought of her rotting alone somewhere almost brought tears to my eyes, but I forced my attention back to a rescue.

There had to be something connecting Travis to his uncle's cabin. A tax bill. A letter. Something, anything with his name on it.

Any minute now. Any minute they'll surround the place, guns drawn, and this whole nightmare will soon be over.

I closed my eyes and waited. Just when I was about to give up, I heard the sound of tires rolling up the driveway.

They're here! They've come for me.

But if I was expecting an army, I would have been disappointed. Instead, there was only the sound of a single car door opening and closing, followed by the jingle of keys as someone entered the cabin.

The police wouldn't have keys.

Travis was back.

More jingling of keys. The door at the top of the stairs swung open, and the sunlight cast his shadow down the creaky wooden stairs.

"Hi, honey," he said. "I'm home. I was thinking we might have pasta for dinner."

I said nothing.

"Okay, pasta it is then."

And the door swung shut.

That's when I began to cry. Only a single tear at first, but soon it was joined by others until they rolled down my cheeks and onto the concrete floor.

I buried my head in my arm and choked back sobs, determined not to let him hear.

FOURTEEN

I dozed off for a while after crying. I woke to the sound of pots and pans up above in the kitchen. The light from the window had faded, and I sat in darkness, listening to Travis sing along to some country song on the radio.

Dante was wrong about the Nine Circles of Hell. There was a tenth circle, and I'd found it there in the basement.

The music stopped, and I heard his keys jiggling in the lock again. The lights flickered on, and I shielded my eyes.

Travis trudged down the stairs with something over his arm. "I brought you a gift. I hope you like it."

The only gift I would like is a one-way bus ticket to somewhere far away from you.

I forced a thin smile across my face. "Oh?"

He held out his arm and displayed the ugliest dress I'd ever seen. It looked as if an 80's teenage prom movie had a love child with Little House on the Prairie. "I had to guess your size. Thought it might be nicer than those pink prison scrubs."

"You expect me to wear that down here in this damp and moldy basement?"

"Oh, I almost forget," he said. "I got some shoes to go along with it. I'll bring them down with dinner."

"How about you give me my Converse back?"

"Those smelly old things? No, you should look like a proper lady."

I imagined how I must have looked and almost laughed—four days since I'd had a shower. No makeup. A bandage on my head, and I was pissing in a bucket.

Like a tacky dress is going to change anything?

"I want my Converse, Travis. And my hoodie. It's cold down here."

"I'll bring you a blanket. But first, why don't you try on the dress? You'll have to be careful with the pasta. It would be a shame to ruin it on the first night."

"I'm not wearing that thing."

The stupid grin disappeared from his face, and his cheeks flushed red. "You will wear it because I said so."

The anger in his voice flickered like the crackle of the fluorescent lights overhead.

"You said it yourself—I don't want to stain such a nice dress with pasta sauce. I'm a messy eater, you know. Always so clumsy."

"Spencer, are you patronizing me?"

"No, it's just—"

"Maybe I don't have a fancy college degree, but I know when someone is putting me on. Now I bought you this dress, spent a pretty penny on it too. How about some fucking gratitude?"

I didn't know what to say. He was clearly upset, and he'd already hit me once. I didn't want him to hit me again.

"Okay," I said. "I'll wear the dress."

The smile returned to his face. "That's better. For a second, I thought you were a bad girl. And well, you know what happens to bad girls."

Bad girls die.

I was beginning to suspect those were more than just empty words.

"Now," he said, "I'm gonna have to unlock the cuffs around your wrists. Promise you'll be a good girl."

My heart quickened, and I worked to keep a straight face. Perhaps this was my chance. I could hit him over the head or strangle him and make a break for it. "Yes," I said. "I promise."

He disappeared up the stairs and came back with a long length of chain, two padlocks, and a heavy wrench. On his way back down the stairs, he stopped to lock the door behind him.

It doesn't matter. He has the key. If I knock him out, I can still get the key.

He took a step toward me, and I pulled back.

"Don't worry. I ain't gonna hurt you."

He took one end of the chain and padlocked it to the shackles between my ankles. Then he padlocked the other end to the wall before placing the key on top of the old washing machine.

"That chain only reaches so far. You get any funny ideas, like trying to knock me over the head or something, and the key will be out of reach. You kill me, and you'll starve down here all alone. So you see, Spencer, it's best you be a good girl and put on the dress. Now hold out your hands."

I wanted to kick. Scream. Spit in his face. But what good would it have done? It was going to take more than feeding him a few lines to get him to drop his guard. No, I'd have to play this game slowly. I did as I was told.

He took the wrench and loosened the bolts on the cuffs around my wrist. Then he slid them free, sliding his fingers along mine with a delicate touch.

"See? That wasn't so hard."

I nodded.

"What? I can't hear you. I need you to say it, Spencer. Was that so hard?"

"No."

"No, what?"

"No, it wasn't so hard."

"That's a good girl. Now take off your shirt and put on the dress." He passed it to me and pulled up the wooden chair, flipped it around, and sat facing me with the back of the chair between his legs.

"You're going to watch me?"

"I'm afraid I don't have any choice. You've been very naughty tonight."

"I can't do it."

"You will do it."

"No, you don't understand. You're supposed to step into a dress, not pull it on over your shoulders. I'm going to need you to take off the shackles too."

He smiled, a stupid little smirk I wanted to slap right off his face. "You'll manage."

Fine.

I started with the filthy pink scrub shirt, left with only an ill-fitting sports bra issued by the jail in Topeka. His eyes moved up and down my body, taking inventory of every mole and curve as I shimmied and slithered into the dress.

As hideous as it was, it turned out to be a perfect fit.

He released a long, slow whistle—the kind construction workers used to make in cheesy movies whenever a pretty girl walked by on the sidewalk. "It's beautiful. Looks like it was made for you."

My skin crawled.

"Aren't you going to say something?"

"Um, thanks."

"You're welcome. You look so nice; it's almost a shame to put the cuffs back on."

Then don't.

But he told me to hold out my hands again, and he slid the cuffs back over them, tightened the bolts down with the wrench.

"Now, the shackles. Those pink pants are ruining the look."

He pulled a different key from his pocket, the same type he'd unlocked my handcuffs with any time I'd had to pee out on the road. One at a time, he released my ankles, the first time they'd been out of the shackles in four days. I rubbed the raw skin before sliding the pants down and kicking them across the floor.

"Perfect. I hope you like garlic in your pasta. I'm a huge fan of garlic."

"Splendid."

Satisfied with my appearance, he reapplied the shackles and disappeared back upstairs. I sat alone in the frigid basement and smoothed the folds and wrinkles of the dress.

It was all so absurd I didn't know whether to laugh or cry. Did he really think I was going to be happy?

Wow, honey. Thanks for the beautiful gift. I'm so looking forward to a romantic dinner.

I wondered if I might be so lucky to get a nice white wine to pair with the pasta. Being chained up in the basement would be a whole lot better if I was drunk.

Dinner was more disastrous than I'd imagined. He tripped and nearly fell as he tiptoed down the stairs with a huge serving tray balanced in both hands. There were pots and plates and even a single yellow daffodil in a plastic vase, but unfortunately, the wine I'd been hoping for was absent.

"Oh wait," he said. "I forgot the shoes."

He practically leaped up the stairs and returned a minute later, clutching a pair of bright pink, shiny pleather heels. "I hope you like them. The lady at the store assured me they matched the dress."

Yeah, if I were a Barbie doll in 1987. Only shoes that ugly could match such a get-up. At least Matt, despite all of his many faults, had impeccable taste.

"Put them on."

I slipped off the jail-issued shoes I'd been wearing and wiggled my toes. After four days without a proper scrub, my feet were more than a little smelly, but he didn't seem to notice or mind.

That's probably because I broke his nose.

I took some pleasure in reliving that moment, the image of blood dripping onto his shirt and the painful wail he'd made as I smashed my feet into his face.

With my outfit complete, it was time to eat. He served the pasta with plastic tongs and poured the sauce over the top. "That's how they do it in Italy," he said. "The sauce always goes on last, or the pasta gets soggy. I watched a few cooking videos. I hope it's tasty."

Under normal circumstances, it would have been cute, maybe even sweet, for a man to cook for me. Matt didn't even know how to use the microwave.

He watched with eager eyes—the same eyes that had watched me undress—as I swirled a plastic fork in the spaghetti and brought it to my lips.

"So?"

"It's good."

"You really think so?"

"Yes." I swirled the fork again and took another bite, careful not to get any sauce on the stupid dress. As much as I hated to admit it, the pasta was actually good. It was the best food I'd had in weeks. If it wasn't for the cuffs around my wrists, I could have been sitting across from a date at a charming restaurant, not squatting on the basement floor with a monster.

"I'm so happy you like it. Just think, I could cook for you like this every night. Wouldn't that be nice?"

I shoved another bite of spaghetti into my mouth and nodded so I wouldn't have to answer directly.

His eyes suddenly grew wide. "Spencer, the dress—"

"What?"

"You've spilled the sauce." He jumped up and paced back and forth, pulling at his hair and mumbling incoherent words under his breath. "It's ruined, Spencer. The beautiful dress I bought for you is ruined."

I looked down and saw a tiny red spot just above my left breast. "It's okay, Travis. It's just a drop or two. I'm sure we can clean it."

"No!" He looked like a boy who'd broken his new toy on Christmas Day. "You ruined it!"

"Do you have any paper towels?"

"Paper towels? That's tomato sauce, Spencer." His eyes became glassy, and I thought he might cry. "It's never going to come out."

I'd seen enough to know Travis ran hot or cold. I was afraid of what could happen when he was running hot.

"Calm down and bring me a rag. The fabric is made of polyester. It'll probably wipe right off."

"Don't tell me to calm down. No, you don't get to do that, not after you ruined the dress. Now dinner is ruined too. I had it all planned. It was supposed to be perfect, and you ruined everything!"

"I'm sorry."

He kicked one of the pots, and red sauce splattered like blood on the wall. "You're not sorry. You wanted this to happen. I knew you didn't like it."

"Travis—"

"Take it off."

"What?"

"I said, take off the fucking dress."

"No, I won't do it."

I knew it wasn't the right thing to say the moment the words left my mouth. He lunged at me and knocked me backward. My still-bandaged head came down hard on the concrete with a loud thump. He paid it no attention. His hands were on me, clawing at the straps of the dress.

"Please, Travis! Please stop." It was my turn to cry. "You're hurting me."

He tore one strap free and then the other. I tried to push him off, but he was too strong. Instead, he slapped me across the jaw and continued clawing. My head, still reeling from the fall, spun, and my body went limp.

It was easy for him now. He took the dress in both hands and tore it down the middle. When he was finished, it lay in tatters beside me.

He left me there on the floor in my underwear, the cold concrete beneath me. For a long time, I stayed very still, listening to the sounds of the floorboards creaking above my head as he continued pacing back and forth upstairs.

I didn't dare move, expecting any moment I would hear his heavy footsteps on the stairs as he returned with a knife in hand to finish what he'd started.

When the pacing stopped, and I thought he might have gone to bed, I sat upright against the wall and rubbed the back of my tender head.

I'm going to die down here. Maybe not tonight. Maybe not tomorrow. But eventually, he's going to kill me.

I told myself not to think about such depressing thoughts—it wouldn't do me any good. But no matter how much I tried, I couldn't force the image of Travis standing above my crumpled and lifeless body from my mind. These things happen—maybe not often—but they do happen. Another pretty girl found dead. Another headline for the six o'clock news. And why not? He'd killed Ruby and Monica. Why should I be any different?

It was a sobering reality check, but rather than dragging me down into despair, I felt a sudden strength.

I'm going to live. I'm going to survive this, whatever it takes, and I'm going to kill him. I'm going to kill him before he kills me first.

I would have laughed if I hadn't been afraid he might hear it. So I sat in silence until from somewhere outside the cabin rose the distant hooting of an owl, drifting in through the window on the cool night air.

Was it the same owl I'd heard the night before, as Travis had dragged me from the van into the basement? It didn't matter. It was a message, a reminder that something still existed beyond these four walls.

I took a few deeps breaths and crawled on my hands and knees into the corner. At the base of the wall, just where it joined the floor, I used the bolt from the cuff around my wrist to carve a single line.

Day one.

FIFTEEN

Time had passed slowly in the van, but at least there had been company and windows with a view of the ever-changing scenery. A small town. A farm with children running and playing in a field. Something to distract the mind as the miles slipped away beneath us.

Now there were only four walls and a single window, through which a beam of bright sunlight illuminated tiny particles of dust.

I spent the morning exploring my space. The chains only allowed me to move a short distance from the wall, but when I dropped my arms behind me and stretched my head toward the center of the room, I glimpsed a vehicle parked outside the window—an old green pickup truck with a rusty chrome bumper—no front license plate.

There were no eggs that morning—no bacon and toast or songs playing on the radio. I thought Travis might have left in the middle of the night until I heard the shuffle of his footsteps moving around above me.

I hoped he would have something else to do besides tending to his captive in the basement. After what seemed like a few hours, there was the jingle of keys at the door and a creaking sound as it swung open.

He slogged down the stairs with a cardboard box in his arms, smiled at me when he reached the bottom. I shivered, and not because it was chilly in the basement, and he'd left me the night before in my underwear.

Oh great, he's brought me another dress.

He frowned when he saw the one he'd torn off me the night before crumpled up into a makeshift pillow. Then he put the box down and took a seat on the chair.

"I'm sorry," he said. "I shouldn't have lost my temper last night."

I was not expecting that. If this is some kind of game, I need to be careful about how I play it.

He didn't wait for me to say anything. "It's just, I want you to be happy with me, and I thought the dress would make you happy."

"It was a beautiful dress, Travis."

He sighed. "We both know you hated it. I was never much use when it came to style or fashion. I just wanted things to be perfect."

"Nothing is ever perfect."

"You are," he said. "You're perfect. That's why I chose you. That's why you're mine."

I'll never be yours.

"How's your head?"

"It's much better." It was a lie, of course, but it was what he wanted to hear. "So, what now?"

He smiled. "I brought you some things. Two blankets and a pillow."

"That's nice of you." I couldn't believe I was thanking him, but after a long, cold night in the basement, a blanket would be a welcome relief.

"And there's more," he said. "Another surprise."

Not another surprise.

"Oh?"

He pulled a sealed plastic bag out of the bottom of the box. I recognized it as the bag the detention deputies had given him in Topeka—the bag with my things.

"I took it from the van before I ditched it. Maybe you'll feel better in your own clothes."

If he hadn't been the monster that he was, I could have kissed him. Nothing would have felt better than to slip into my jeans and hoodie.

"I'll wash them for you," he said as he nodded toward the old washer and dryer. "In the meantime, maybe you'd like to take a hot bath?"

I was wrong. A hot bath would be even better than my hoodie.

I nodded. As much as I wanted—no, needed—to clean myself up, I imagined Travis perched on the toilet, watching me with a grin on his face as I bathed.

As if reading my thoughts, he said, "Don't worry. I'll be a gentleman. You can have the bathroom to yourself, as long as you promise to behave."

"I promise." The words came out of me like some obedient, 1950's housewife, but I'd already decided after the events of last night, it would be better to play nice. Maybe if

I could get him to trust me, he'd let his guard down. Maybe then I'd have a chance to kill him.

"Great, a hot bath it is then."

He tore open the plastic bag and threw the contents into the washer, placing my black Converse shoes neatly on top. I was surprised when the old machine sputtered and came to life. It looked as though it hadn't been used in a decade or two.

With the clothes in the wash, he went upstairs and came back with the wrench, loosened the bolts on the cuffs and my hands slid free.

"The shackles stay on," he said as he slid his arm around my elbow. "Be careful on the stairs."

It was my first time seeing the cabin. It was modest, not much more than two or three rooms with old furnishings to match the washer and dryer. I was most surprised by how neat and tidy everything was. In the kitchen, a dishrag was draped neatly over the door handle of a vintage stove. The pots and pans from last night had been washed and returned, in order of smallest to biggest, to the open shelves of a wooden cupboard.

"Do you like it?"

"Huh?" I was distracted by the wood-burning stove in the living room. How nice it would have been in the winter to curl up beside it with a good book.

"The cabin? Do you like it? I know it's not much."

"It's—quaint."

He must have been satisfied with my answer because he smiled as he led me into the bathroom and turned the tap above a deep, clawfoot tub.

"There's soap and shampoo there, on the rack beside the toilet. You can undress as soon as I lock the door behind me. Oh, and Spencer?"

"Yeah?"

"Wash your feet real good. I didn't want to say anything last night, but they stink."

Maybe I didn't bust his nose as bad as I thought.

It didn't matter. The only thing that mattered at the moment was the pure bliss of slipping my cold and achy body into the steamy hot water. There was even a bottle of bubble bath. I poured a capful into the water, and soon the shackles on my ankles were hidden beneath a layer of thick, lavender-scented foam. I could have been any other girl in any other place.

But you're not just any other girl.

He was playing nice today. It was a part of his twisted plan, like good cop and bad cop, designed to break me down until I would do anything he said. But I wasn't going to let myself be fooled. I had a plan too. I just wasn't sure how I was going to pull it off.

I unwrapped the bandage on my head and touched the place where he'd hit me the first night. A small scab had formed, and the wound was clean. It stung only a little as I massaged shampoo onto my scalp and into my hair, which I washed twice until it was soft and clean. Then came the soap. I scrubbed and scrubbed until the dirt had been worked free from my knees and elbows before moving on to the rest of my body. I'd just finished scrubbing between my toes when a knock came at the door.

"Spencer?"

"I'm almost finished."

"Take your time," he said, his voice slightly muffled by the door. "I'm going to open up and leave a clean towel on the toilet seat—just a crack. I won't peak. Knock on the door whenever you're ready, and I'll come for you."

I'll come for you.

Travis always had a way of making everything sound creepy. Maybe that's why he'd decided to kidnap me. He was too creepy to meet a girl under normal circumstances. Then again, Matt wasn't creepy at all when we met. He'd turned out to be a totally different kind of psycho.

I wanted to stay in the tub forever until I'd shriveled up so small I could slip right out through the drain. I added more hot water and had almost dozed off when he knocked on the door again.

"I've got coffee," he said. "And toast."

I knew it was his way of telling me he'd become impatient, so I climbed awkwardly from the tub—it wasn't easy with the shackles—and dried myself off with the towel. When I'd wrapped it securely around my body, I rapped my knuckles on the door and waited for him to come.

He led me into the living room and took a seat next to me on the sofa. "Your clothes are in the dryer."

"Was I in the tub that long?"

"Nearly an hour. Would you like some coffee?"

"Yes, black."

He disappeared into the kitchen and came back with coffee and toast on a Mickey Mouse tray. We drank and ate, and I thought about how surreal it was to be drinking coffee with my kidnapper—the murderer of my friend.

When the coffee was finished, we went back down to the basement, where we repeated the same process we'd done with the dress. I pulled on my t-shirt and hoodie before he returned my wrists to the cuffs chained to the wall. Only then did he remove the shackles just long enough for me to pull on my skinny jeans.

"It's nice," he said, passing me the Converse and watching as I slid them onto my feet. "You look natural, like the kind of girl who'd be comfortable in the city or roasting marshmallows around a campfire."

"Thanks." I was just glad to be back in my own clothes, with a hoodie and two blankets to keep me warm.

He snapped his fingers. "Hey, I have an idea. Why don't we cook dinner together tonight? There's a recipe for roast chicken I've been wanting to try—garlic, herb, and butter."

"That sounds great."

He winked. "Pick you up at seven."

I'm looking forward to it.

And it was true, I was looking forward to it. A kitchen has knives. And a knife was what I needed to kill him.

SIXTEEN

If someone had been standing outside the cabin looking in through a window, they would have seen a happy, young couple preparing dinner together. They would have seen a man chopping carrots and chives and a woman pressing cloves of garlic as they both sang along to the radio. They would have seen lit candles on the table and thought it was all very romantic. And then they would have moved on, never knowing the real truth of what they'd seen.

As promised, he came for me at seven. He'd spent hours before in preparation. I'd heard him moving things back and forth from the kitchen to the living room. At one point, he even went out to his truck, and I thought he might have left, but minutes later, he was back, pacing around above me as little clumps of dust fell from the basement ceiling.

By the time he'd led me up to the kitchen, there was already a raw chicken sitting alone in a glass dish on top of the stove. Vegetables and other ingredients were lined up neatly in plastic bags.

He placed his hands on my shoulders and looked me in the eyes. "Can I trust you?"

"Yes."

He surveyed me suspiciously. Perhaps I'd hesitated a second too long with my reply. Then he brought his hands in front of his chest and rubbed them together. "Good, because the kitchen can be a very dangerous place. But just in case, I've removed all of the knives and pointy objects and put them in my truck for safekeeping."

I did my best to appear confused. "But how will we chop the vegetables?"

He pulled back one side of his flannel shirt to reveal a small knife hanging from his belt in a leather sheath. "I'll do the chopping. You can help with everything else. There's a garlic press over there. Start with that."

Damnit. There has to be something else in the kitchen I can kill him with.

I did as I was told and got to work on the garlic. When I was sure his back was turned, I glanced around the room, desperate to find something that might make a suitable deadly weapon.

No luck.

There was time, I told myself. Better to let him relax and become too comfortable. So I pressed garlic and waited and laughed at his bad attempts to be funny.

"Hold up," he said. "Something isn't right. You're not having any fun."

"Sure, I am. It's nice to spend some time out of the basement."

"No, that's not what I meant."

What is it now?

"We need some music? Don't you think we need some music?"

"Um, I guess so."

He carried a small, portable radio in from the living room and plugged it into an outlet behind the counter. "I'm afraid there's only one channel way out here. Let's see what we've got."

He fidgeted with the dial for a minute and picked up a signal. A bouncing disco beat filled the small space of the kitchen. I recognized the song immediately: Stayin' Alive by the Bee Gees.

Travis hummed along with words as if the irony of the lyrics was totally lost on him. Even I joined in here and there if only to play the part of a girl who was somehow having fun.

By the time we'd finished with the preparations and put the chicken in the oven, the radio had moved on to Gloria Gaynor's I Will Survive.

I wondered if it was a conspiracy, as if the disc jockey at the radio station was a part of some sick, cosmic joke. Or maybe it was the universe just telling me what I needed to hear.

I sang along at the top of my lungs, holding a wooden spoon like a microphone. "Go on now, go, walk out the door. Just turn around now, 'cause you're not welcome anymore!"

Once again, the words seemed lost on Travis, who didn't seem to pay them any mind. Instead, he smiled and hummed along as I sang.

When the song had finished, he gave me a lighter and told me to light the candles on the kitchen table. Then he took two glasses down from the cupboard.

"I have a surprise for you."

Please, no more surprises.

He went to the refrigerator and pulled out a bottle of white wine. "I read it goes well with chicken. I'm sorry I don't have any proper wine glasses."

It was just some cheap off-brand label, but it didn't matter. Suddenly I felt very thirsty. "That's very thoughtful, Travis. Why don't you serve it?"

I hoped he might pull a corkscrew out of a drawer, something I'd later be able to stab into his neck, but instead, the cap twisted off, and he poured us each a glass.

We sat at the table and sipped chilled wine as the kitchen slowly filled with the scent of garlic and herbs and simmering chicken. Candle flames danced and flickered between us. And for a moment, any anger I'd felt toward him was replaced by a kind of pity.

Travis wasn't ugly. Out of his uniform, he was almost handsome. Yes, he'd shown a violent temper, but in his better moments, he'd proven he was capable of thoughtful and gentle consideration. He was even neat and tidy, but not in an obsessive way like Matt.

So why did he think the only way to get a girlfriend was to kidnap one? It was sad, really. Was he a monster? A psychopath? Or maybe the product of a deranged mother?

Either way, it was too late for him now. He'd become a serial murderer, and for that, there were no second chances, no redemption.

We finished the first glass, and he poured us each another. It had been an hour since we'd put the chicken in the oven, and the timer still read thirty minutes. With only toast for breakfast, I was hungry. Even the small amount of wine had already gone to my head.

By the time we pulled the chicken from the oven, we'd emptied the bottle. Travis produced a second bottle and offered me another glass.

Keep drinking. If I'm feeling it, that means he'll be feeling it too.

I drank my wine as he sliced the chicken and carried two plates to the table. Like the spaghetti the night before, it was delicious—well-seasoned and tender enough to cut with the plastic knives and forks he'd set the table with.

"Tell me about your childhood," he said. "In the van, you mentioned something about foster care."

I didn't want to talk about my childhood, least of all my dead mother. "It's nothing special, really. Let's just say life wasn't easy."

"I'm sorry about that."

"What about your family?"

"Oh, my father wasn't around much. And my mother—" He gazed off for a moment as if lost in thought. "Let's just say my mother can be a lot to deal with."

So there it was. Deadbeat dad. Controlling mother. The perfect recipe for a grade-A psychopath. Although it wasn't an excuse, plenty of people with shitty parents turned out just fine. I'd had a deadbeat dad too and had never killed anyone. At least not yet.

Soon enough.

"Well," he said. "That's all behind us now. We can build a new life together, Spencer. Just you and me. Whatever you want, I'll find a way to give it to you."

"Right now, I'd like some more wine. How about you?"

He started to stand, and I placed my hand over his forearm. "Sit," I said. "I'll pour the wine. This has all been so wonderful. You've already done so much."

He smiled and relaxed in his chair. I took our glasses and went to the counter, emptied the rest of the bottle, and took a deep breath.

I swung in a big arc, holding the bottle firmly by the neck, and brought it down onto his head.

"You bitch!" He slid from the chair and rolled onto the floor, one hand raised to his bleeding head and the other grabbing onto the chain between my ankles. "I'll kill you! I'll fucking kill you."

He jerked hard, and I fell to the floor beside him, still clutching the unbroken bottle in my fingers. I swung again and missed. He knocked the bottle from my hand, and it went spinning into the corner.

I tried to claw myself away from him, but he pulled me closer until his hands, now covered in blood, wrapped around my neck.

He was crying. "I would have given you everything. Everything! And you ruined it. You ruin everything." Tears mixed with blood and ran down his lips, tiny droplets splattering my face as he spoke.

"Travis—"

His hands squeezed harder and harder until I couldn't breathe. There was only one thing left to do. I reached down to his belt and pulled the knife from its sheath, raising it above my head and bringing it down with all of my strength.

He released a hand from my neck and tried to block my attack, but it was too late. The knife sunk deep into his shoulder, and he screamed.

It was the only chance I was going to get. I scrambled to my feet as he lay moaning and wailing on the floor, the handle of the knife still sticking out of his shoulder.

"No," he said. "Please don't go. I'll forget everything. Just stay. Oh, please stay. I need help, Spencer. You can't leave me like this."

"I will leave you. Just like you left Ruby." I turned to walk out, but not before knocking the candles over and watching as the tablecloth caught fire.

There was still the problem of the shackles around my ankles. I wanted to go back for the key. Maybe it was in one of his pockets. But I couldn't risk him getting his hands on me again. If he did, it would all be over.

Instead, I shuffled out the front door as fast as I could manage and started down the gravel drive, turning only once to look back at the cabin. An orange glow was visible in the kitchen window, and I wondered how long it would be before the cabin was engulfed in flames.

The drive wound its way through a dark forest. The alcohol was not helping, and I tripped more than one time as I shuffled along. It was quiet now, only the sound of crickets chirping and the chain clinking between my feet.

It seemed to go on forever, and I wondered how long it might be until I reached the road. I was tired, and my thighs hurt from all the shuffling, but I didn't dare stop to catch my breath. I imagined he might be somewhere behind me in the dark, still clutching his bleeding shoulder, intent on catching up with me and finishing me off like he'd done to poor Ruby.

Something flashed in front of me, a flutter moving out of the trees and over the gravel drive before disappearing again into the blackness of night. From somewhere nearby, I heard the familiar hoot. It was the owl, come to wish me luck perhaps, or warn me of dangers yet to come.

Finally, after what seemed like hours spent shuffling along in the dark, I reached a two-lane county road.

Which way should I go?

I didn't even know which state I was in, let alone how close the nearest town or wayward gas station might be. In one direction, the road went up, winding along the side of the mountain. In the other direction, it went down.

I chose down, figuring towns were usually in valleys. If there wasn't a town, then a farm or ranch house maybe. It didn't matter, as long as there was someone, anyone, who could help me.

And so I shuffled down the road, tripping here and there, without so much as a car or the light of a warm house in sight. But no matter how tired I felt, I kept going, pulling my black hoodie around me to shield against the cool mountain air.

Hours passed without a sign of life, and I became increasingly desperate. If I could just hold out until morning, until the light of day, maybe a car would pass, and I'd be saved.

That's when I saw the headlights approaching, beams of light penetrating the darkness.

My first instinct was to hide. But I was so awfully tired. I was certain my ankles were bleeding. And I wasn't sure how much longer I would be able to go on. I had to take the chance, no matter how risky it might have been.

"Help!" I stood in the middle of the road, waving my arms above me and signaling for the approaching vehicle to stop. "Oh, please help! I've been kidnapped. You have to help me!"

The car slowed to a stop, the cool night mist reflecting in the headlights. It wasn't until they switched off that I recognized the rusty chrome bumper and saw him smiling at from behind the windshield. I screamed.

"Hello, Spencer." Travis stepped out from behind the driver-side door with a bloody rag wrapped around his shoulder. "You've been a very, very bad girl. Now, what are we going to have to do about that?"

I took a step backward and tripped, crawled along the rough pavement in a desperate attempt to get away.

It wasn't long before his weight was on top of me, jerking my arms behind my back and snapping a pair of handcuffs around my wrists. Then he picked me up and threw me, kicking and screaming, over his uninjured shoulder.

I thought he might kill me right there, toss me over the guardrail and into the ditch the same as he'd done to Ruby. But instead, he dropped me into the back of the pickup and started up the road toward the cabin. I wondered if maybe it would have been better to die than to find myself back in the basement. At least if I died, I would be free of the pain, free of him. But Travis had other plans.

I'd spent hours shuffling along in the darkness, but in the truck, it took only a few minutes to reach the cabin. As he carried me inside and toward the basement, I noticed the blackened walls of the kitchen, no doubt from the fire I'd set ablaze.

He didn't even wait until we were all the way down the stairs before tossing me from his shoulder. My chin slammed into one of the steps and busted open. Blood ran down my neck and stained my hoodie.

Then he grabbed me by my ankles and dragged me, still bleeding, into the corner. I already knew what would happen next. The cuffs tightened around my wrists. I was trapped, once again a prisoner in this place where I was ever more certain I would eventually die.

He took a seat on the chair and pulled back the bloody rag from his shoulder. "It was all going so well, Spencer. Now just look at what you've done."

Please, just leave. Leave me alone.

I couldn't stand the sight of his face. "Are you going to kill me?"

His face twisted up like he was considering my question. "I should kill you, especially after what you've done. But that would be too easy. It's like I told you, Spencer, you are mine. And I'm never going to let you go."

I spit in his direction, a big mess of phlegm and blood that landed at his feet.

He laughed. "Now, that's not very nice. But you'll come around after you've had some time to think about what you've done."

Maybe it was what he'd said, or the wine, or the blow to my chin, but I suddenly felt very sick. I crawled to the bucket and vomited, my stomach heaving in and out with each retch.

"That's good," he said. "Get it out." Then he stood and flicked off the light before limping up the stairs.

I hovered over the bucket for a long time until I was sure there was nothing more left. Then I crawled into the corner and scratched another line next to the one I'd made the night before.

Day two.

I didn't know if I'd survive one more.

SEVENTEEN

I hovered over the bucket and retched up the contents of my stomach again. The smell of vomit and bile still lingered from the night before, and my stomach twisted up in knots.

It was mid-morning when the door at the top of the stairs opened. Travis appeared with his flannel shirt unbuttoned, a clean bandage over his shoulder.

"Spencer," he said with the tone of a middle school math teacher speaking to a failing student, "what am I going to do with you?"

"I hate you." The words erupted from my lips. It wasn't smart to risk setting him off, but I couldn't think of anything better to say. "You're a monster."

He cocked his head to one side and considered me for a long moment. "Oh, then I guess you don't want this bottle of water."

I was desperate. My throat was dry and scratchy from all of the vomiting, and I caved. "I'm sorry. Please, I'm so thirsty."

"That's better." He smiled and placed the bottle on the ground between us before taking a step back.

I struggled against the chains to reach it. My hands were too far behind me to pick it up, so I wrapped my lips around the cap and dragged it into the corner. I felt like an animal but quickly forgot my humiliation when the cool water soothed my aching throat.

"Go easy," he said. "That's all your getting today. I'm going to give you some time to think about what you've done."

"Please, Travis. I'm sorry. I'm just scared, okay? You're scaring me."

He scoffed. "Why should you be afraid of me? I love you, Spencer. I told you that. I'll always love you."

You're not capable of love, Travis. You're a psychopath.

"I love you too," I said. It was a lie, of course.

He brought his lips together and made a clicking sound. "See, that's the thing. I don't think you do. At least not yet. But you will. Believe me, you will."

At least he's not planning to kill me. Not yet.

"Rest now," he said, turning his back to me and heading toward the stairs. "We've got a long journey ahead of us, you and I."

"Wait, aren't you going to empty the bucket?"

He only laughed.

Three days passed this way. The bucket had filled near to the brim with vomit and urine and things best left unmentioned. Each day, he brought me only a single bottle of water. And as the hunger in my stomach grew, I become weaker. By the fourth day, I was delirious.

The only measure of my sanity was the line I carved into the corner every night. Once, I'd nearly forgotten until the hooting of the owl reminded me of my duty.

"Be strong," I heard him say.

And so I crawled into the corner and scratched my line before sleep finally overtook me.

A week had come and gone since he'd first brought me here. Outside, in the busy world of jobs and coffee with friends and a twenty-four-hour media cycle, a week might not seem like much. It comes and goes with as much consideration as what to watch on Netflix. But in Travis' basement, a week was an eternity.

He appeared that morning with the usual water and something else. I smelled it the moment he came down the stairs—a plate of toast, which he set down on the ground before me.

I ate greedily as he watched, unashamed as I shoveled the toast into my mouth with filthy fingers. Maybe I no longer care what he thought, or maybe I was just so hungry I would have eaten scraps from a dumpster.

I licked any remaining crumbs from the plate as he pulled up the chair, spinning it around and sitting with the back between his legs as was his usual custom.

"In China," he said, "the people tell an old folktale about a clever man named Liang. It's a wonderful story. Have you heard it?"

I wondered how a man like Travis had come to know a Chinese folktale. "No," I said. "I've never heard it."

He smiled. "Liang is a common man, a peasant really, who makes wooden toys for the children in the village. One day, he sees a beautiful princess, the daughter of the emperor, and decides he will marry her.

"But Liang's father laughs at him. After all, he was born of humble stock. Why should the emperor's daughter marry a simple peasant boy?

"Now, in those days, dragons roamed the countryside. One particularly nasty dragon lived in a cave near Liang's village. Several times a year, the dragon would swoop down on the village. He ate pigs, water buffalo, and any people unlucky enough to be around. The emperor had done nothing about it until one day, the dragon burned the fields with fire.

"The people were despondent and pleaded with the emperor to dispatch the dragon once and for all. And so the emperor promised his daughter's hand in marriage to any man who could vanquish the terrible dragon."

I listened as he spoke. I was still hungry despite the toast and hoped if I played along with his game, he'd bring me more food before the day was up.

"Liang knew this was his only chance. He worked for three days and nights, carving a giant dragon's head from wood. When it was finished, he carried it to the evil dragon's cave and placed it on a rock outside the entrance so that it looked like the rest of the dragon's body was hidden behind the rock. Then Liang gave a mighty roar, and soon the evil dragon appeared.

"The evil dragon rushed from his cave. 'Who goes there?' But the wooden dragon only glared back at him with menacing eyes. And so the evil dragon wondered why the other was not afraid and thought he must surely be a very dangerous foe. 'I'm leaving for a while,' he said, as he spread his wings and flew away. 'Make yourself at home in my cave.' For you see, the evil dragon was really a coward and had no will to fight.

"Liang was celebrated in the village as a hero. And the emperor, true to his word, gave Liang his daughter's hand in marriage. The couple lived happily ever after, and people came from miles around to buy Liang's wooden toys."

Travis waited a long time for me to respond, looking at me as though I'd somehow missed the point. To be honest, I wasn't exactly sure what point he was trying to make.

"Don't you get it?" he said.

"Get what?"

"Liang was a humble and poor man, but still, he found a way to marry the emperor's beautiful daughter."

"No," I said. "I still don't get it."

"If Liang can marry the emperor's daughter, then it means one day I'll marry you."

I thought I might vomit the toast back up. "But what about the daughter, Travis? Did she have any say in deciding who to marry? Did she even want to marry Liang?"

He looked confused like he'd never considered the story from the daughter's perspective. It was like that with men, always assuming the damsel in distress would succumb to their valor and bravery. As if women were nothing more than secondary characters in their world.

"No, you're missing the point. Liang found a way, Spencer. Just like I'm going to find a way. You'll see. Someday we'll be happy."

It was a nice thought, and if it was enough to keep me alive, I'd go along with it. I imagined myself in the distant future picking flowers in our garden, shackles still wrapped around my ankles.

"I tried." He threw his hands up and winced at the pain in his bandaged shoulder. "And I'll keep trying. I'll never give up on you."

That's what I'm afraid of.

I watched him trudge back up the stairs and was glad to be alone. At least the toast had settled my aching stomach, though the stench from the near-overflowing bucket wasn't doing much to help.

I didn't wait until nightfall to carve my line that day. It had become a ritual, something that gave me strength, so I moved on my hands and knees to the corner and used the bolt on my cuffs to scrape away at the concrete.

I was nearly finished when a piece of the wall, no bigger than a quarter, crumbled away and fell to the ground. I brushed the exposed concrete with my finger. It was soft. Waterlogged. Decayed.

Nothing lasts forever.

An idea came to me. I traced my fingers along the wall to the place where the heavy chains from my wrists joined an o-ring, sunk deep into the wall with an even larger bolt.

I took the chain in both hands and pulled up, then down. The bolt didn't budge. It was useless, I thought. But I tried again and was surprised when a small amount of the concrete, no more than dust, fell away from the wall. Again I jiggled the chain, and this time a bigger piece, no larger than a fingernail, flecked and fell to the floor. I crouched down to pick it up.

It had fallen into a narrow crack between the slab floor and the wall, and as I felt around for it, my fingers found something else wedged into the tiny space.

It took some doing, but eventually, I worked it loose from the crack and held it in front of my face. It was a single tooth, stained with blood.

I would have screamed—at least the Spencer from a week ago would have screamed. But I knew he was above me, lurking somewhere in the cabin. I had to be strong, hold my secrets close, and not give them away if I had any chance of surviving.

I turned the tooth over in my hand. That's when I knew, beyond any doubt, that I wasn't the first girl to wind up in Travis' basement. He'd played this game before.

I stayed awake long past midnight, just enough light shining in through the high window for me to see the tooth I still clutched in my hand. I wondered what had become of her. Did her ghost linger there in the darkness? Was she watching me now, hoping that I might find a way to free myself, and in doing so, finally set her free?

"I'm sorry," I whispered to the empty room. "Whatever it was that happened to you, I'm so sorry."

I was sorry. I imagined her chained to the wall, no different than myself, hoping that any moment help would come to rescue her. But it hadn't come for her, and it wouldn't come for me.

I would have to save myself.

I put the tooth in my pocket, vowing that if I ever escaped this place, I'd give it to the authorities. I didn't know much about DNA evidence, but I remembered reading somewhere about dental records being used to match the remains of victims to their identities. Perhaps there was a family somewhere, still wondering what had happened to their daughter, their sister, their niece. Maybe I could give them some kind of closure, put to rest whatever doubts and questions still lingered in the back of their minds. The thought bolstered my resolve. It gave me something to live for besides myself.

And so when hours passed without a footstep from above, when I was certain he was asleep, I stood again and took the chain in my hands. I yanked up and down, taking care not to make too much noise. The bolt didn't budge.

It was okay, I told myself. I had to keep trying. If only I kept trying, it might loosen enough for me to escape, if not now or tomorrow, then maybe the next day. The next week. The next month. However long it might take, I would earn my freedom.

Four inches of metal. Maybe six. And some old, decaying concrete. That was all that stood between me and escape from the monster who lay sleeping upstairs.

I worked long into the night, careful not to make too much noise. I worked until I grew tired, but it didn't matter. I'd found some purpose, and it was better than feeling sorry for myself. Better than playing the helpless girl.

I worked until I could stay awake no longer. As I pulled the blankets around me and prepared for sleep, the hooting of the owl came again from beyond the window. He was speaking to me. Only this time, he said, "Don't give up."

I dreamed again that night. Not of the lake, with its invisible hands pulling me down, or being buried alive in a wooden box. I dreamed I was walking alone along some rugged Pacific beach, staring out over the waves as they crashed into jagged rocks.

I dreamed I was finally free.

EIGHTEEN

The next morning, he brought toast and salty scrambled eggs. I licked the plate clean as he told me another story about a young man who was in love with the daughter of a loathsome Turkish sultan. Her jealous father had locked her away in a tower on an island in the Bosporus. Each night, her young lover would swim the treacherous waters, risking sharks and the sultan's wrath to reach her.

"That's a lovely story," I said.

"Don't you want to know how it ends?"

"Um, I guess so."

"He dies," he said. "One night, the boy emerged from the water to find the sultan and his soldiers standing guard over the tower. They killed him and threw his body into the current. He was swept out to the Mediterranean Sea. And each night, the girl wept for him until she grew old in her tower and died."

I wasn't sure what to say. "It's a sad story. I don't think I understand."

"It's not that hard," he said. "You're the sultan's daughter, locked in a tower."

No, Travis. I'm chained up in your basement.

"And I'm the young boy, swimming across treacherous waters night after night to reach my love. Nothing, not even sharks, could keep me from you."

If you're the boy, then I like the part when he dies.

He pushed the chair back and stood. "I'm going into town for another supply run. I'll be back in a few hours."

At least it meant he would leave me alone. I waited until I heard the sound of his old truck starting up and tires rolling down the drive. When I was sure he was gone, I got back to work on the bolt.

In an hour, my fingers were sore, so I wrapped the chain with a blanket and kept swinging up and down, and more flecks of concrete fell away from the wall.

The bolt must have been set deep. Despite my efforts, it wouldn't budge. Still, I wouldn't lose hope. It was like that movie, Shawshank Redemption, where the lead character spent years digging a hole through his cell wall with a tiny rock pick. I would never give up, not until I was free of this place and had my revenge on Travis.

My work was interrupted by the sound of a vehicle approaching the cabin. It had been less than two hours, not long enough for Travis to make it all the way into town and back. I dropped the blanket and leaned against the chains until I caught a glimpse of the vehicle out of the tiny window.

It wasn't Travis' truck. It was a passenger car, a faded and off-putting shade of red.

I wanted to scream for help, but I wasn't sure it was a good idea. I'd grown more cautious during my days in the basement and decided to wait until I could be certain it wasn't someone who might do me harm.

Upstairs, I heard the front door open, followed by footsteps on the wooden floorboards.

"Oh, my lord! What happened here?" It was a woman's voice. I guessed she was older, maybe fifty or sixty. Perhaps she's seen the charred walls of the kitchen.

"What has that boy done? I swear, he'll never learn."

It's his mother. Or an aunt, maybe. No, only a mother could talk about her own son that way.

"Please! I'm down here. You have to come and help me. Oh, please help me!"

The footsteps stopped.

"Down here," I screamed. "I'm down here in the basement."

Several minutes passed before the footsteps resumed. I heard the rustling of pots and pans, glasses being taken down from the cupboard.

In another few minutes, there was the jingling of keys, and the basement door opened. A woman, heavyset, struggled as she lowered herself down the stairs. In her hands, she carried the same Mickey Mouse serving tray, two steaming mugs of some hot liquid on top.

"Please," I said. "He's trapped me down here. You have to help me. I don't know how much longer I'm going to make it."

"Now, now, honey." Her voice had a peculiar accent I couldn't place, Southern maybe. "Just calm yourself. No use getting your panties all in a bunch. I made tea. Would you like some?"

"No, I don't want any tea. Do you have the keys? You must have the keys." I held up my hands so she could see the cuffs around my wrists. "There's a wrench upstairs. Oh, please help me before he comes back."

She seemed entirely oblivious to my plight. I thought maybe she was senile. I'd spent a summer working in a nursing home and had seen firsthand the effects dementia had on the elderly.

She placed a mug on the ground in front of me, careful not to come too close, then took a seat on the chair.

She sipped from her mug. "What's your name, honey?"

"Spencer," I said. "Spencer Madison."

"You a girl, ain't you?"

"Can't you see what's happening?" I wondered how long it might be before Travis returned. "I'm a prisoner. Travis kidnapped me."

Her face remained completely unchanged as if my words had failed to register. "Kind of a funny name for a girl, don't you think?"

My pleas for help weren't working, so I took the tea in my hands and sipped. "Yes, ma'am. I get that a lot. What's your name?"

"Henrietta," she said, "on account of my father's name was Henry. Never did like the name very much."

"Well, Henrietta, there's a wrench upstairs. Do you think you could find it for me?"

"Oh no, he wouldn't be very happy if I did that."

"Who? Who wouldn't be happy?"

"My Travis."

So she is the mother.

"I told him not to bring another girl here. But he's never listened to me, that boy. Not even when he was shitting in diapers."

"Another girl?"

"Oh, honey. You don't really think you're the first girl he's ever fallen in love with? You're pretty. I'll give you that. Even if you do have a boy's name."

I already knew from the tooth I'd found in the crack I wasn't the first. What was even more shocking was that his own mother seemed to know about the things he'd done.

She took another sip of her tea. "I have to say I was a bit surprised to hear you down here. I wasn't expecting he'd find one so soon—not after the last mess. Oh, it took me ages to clean up all the blood. But what good is a mother if not to look after her son?"

It was clear she wasn't going to rescue me. I'd need a different strategy. "But I love him," I said. "I love Travis."

"Liar!" She threw her mug on the floor, and it shattered into a thousand pieces.

"It's true."

"No one could ever love my son. He's a monster. Came right out of the womb that way, screaming and gnawing at my tits with those filthy little gums from the day he was born."

"So then why do you help him?"

She looked around at the scattered pieces of the broken mug and sighed. "Now, look what you've made me do. I was really enjoying that tea."

"I'm sorry," I said. "But you didn't answer my question, Henrietta. Can I call you Henrietta?"

She nodded.

"If he's such a monster, why do you help him?"

"It's simple," she said. "I'm his mother. I wouldn't expect you to understand."

I couldn't argue with the logic of her answer. "You know, there's more than one way to help Travis. He's sick, Henrietta. He needs the care of professionals."

"You mean head shrinkers?"

"No, I mean people trained to take care of someone like him. There are places he could go."

Places where they'd lock him up and throw away the key.

"You want me to send my boy away? Lock him up in the funny farm with the mouth breathers and droolers? Oh no, I don't think so."

"Maybe there's another option. Why don't you help me out of the basement, and we'll make you another cup of tea, figure things out together?"

"I don't like you," she said. "You're a city girl—the kind of folks who think they're better and smarter than us country bumpkins. And you talk too much."

I was about to prove her point by speaking again when I heard another set of tires crunching over the gravel in the driveway.

Is Travis back so soon?

Henrietta stood and went over to the window. I could tell from the look of surprise that crossed her face, it was not Travis in the driveway. It was someone else, someone she hadn't been expecting.

There was a knock on the front door and a voice calling out from the porch. "Hello? It's Sheriff Johnson. Henrietta? Travis? Is anyone home?"

She leaped from the chair and flung herself at me, bringing her fat hand over my mouth before I had a chance to scream. "Shush, girl. Don't you dare make a sound, or I'll kill you myself."

The front door swung open, and I heard footsteps above in the living room.

"Henrietta? I saw your car in the driveway. You down in the basement?"

Henrietta whispered in my ear. "Be a good girl now, and don't cause no problems. Be a good girl, and nobody has to get hurt."

She released her grip and started up the stairs, taking care to close the door gently behind her. I leaned forward, struggling to make out their conversation.

"Sheriff? I wasn't expecting you," she said.

"Oh, Jim Tanner in town said Travis had come by the store a few days back, and he saw your car over at Fleming's Beauty Parlor this morning." The sheriff's voice was warm and friendly, not the voice of someone who suspected a kidnapping victim was stashed away right beneath his boots. "Figured you two might be staying up here at the cabin. Listen, we've had quite a few mountain lion sightings this year. I wanted to come by and warn you myself."

"Mountain lions? Oh, good heavens. Well, Travis has a shotgun. I'm sure we'll be fine. I don't have much to eat, or I'd offer you something, and well, I'm terribly busy with the laundry."

"Oh, that's alright," he said. "Don't want to trouble you folks none. You say hello to Travis for me."

It was my only chance. I threw my head back and screamed. "Help! I'm down here. They've kidnapped me. Please, help me!"

"Now, what in the hell is that?"

I heard the shuffling of his boots moving closer to the basement door.

"Oh, it's that old washer," she said. "Makes such terrible noises."

"The washer?" said the sheriff. His voice had changed into something more serious. "Henrietta, you got someone down in the basement?"

I screamed again.

"Zeke Johnson," she said, "don't you open that door."

"Sit down, Henrietta. And keep your hands where I can see them."

The door opened to reveal a thin man holding a large revolver in both hands. He was old, maybe in his sixties or even seventies, with a grey beard that framed his slender, chiseled face.

His eyes grew wide as he caught sight of me. "Sweet Jesus."

"They're going to kill me," I said. "Please, you have to help me."

He took a few cautious steps down the stairs, his gun still pointed in front of him. "Don't you worry, darling. It's okay now. Sheriff Johnson is here."

My body went limp. It was over. Help had come. There was still the case in Portland and the threats Matt had made the night I'd fled with his car, but at least I'd be free of Travis and the basement. Tears welled up in my eyes and rolled down my cheeks. "Thank you," I said. "Thank you."

He scanned the room as he neared the bottom of the stairs, his gaze jumping between the bucket of puke and piss and the chains around my wrists. "In all my years—"

I didn't have time to warn him. Henrietta came racing down the stairs with the kind of quickness I'd never seen in someone her age. I'd only opened my mouth to scream when she brought a large frying pan crashing down on the back of his head. He stumbled forward and fell face-first down the remaining stairs. There was a loud crack as he hit the floor, and blood oozed from his mouth.

That's when Travis appeared at the top of the stairs, still holding a bag of groceries in each hand. "Oh, mama. What have you done?"

NINETEEN

"It wasn't me," she said. "It was the girl. She screamed, Travis. I had no choice. She made me do it."

He'd put the grocery bags down and was standing with his mother at the bottom of the stairs. "What are you doing here?"

"I saw you on the news. They said your partner had been killed, and the van you were driving went missing. They said you might be dead too, murdered by two fugitives from justice. But I knew, Travis. You're my son. I knew."

He lowered his head like a little boy being scolded by the teacher. "I'm sorry, mama."

She turned and pointed in my direction. "So soon? You know what happened to the last one."

Just then, the sheriff gasped for air and choked on the blood between his lips.

"Oh, heck," she said. "I thought I'd killed him."

Travis stomped up the stairs and came back with a plastic grocery bag.

The poor sheriff's eyes had the same expression as the deer I'd hit in Matt's Audi, just before it bounced off the hood of the car.

"Please," he said, blood spurting out of his mouth.

But it was too late.

Travis pulled the plastic bag over the old man's head and held it tight. In another minute, it was all over.

"We both killed him," said Henrietta. "Now, you're gonna help me clean this up."

"What do we do, mama?"

He was no longer the man I'd seen bossing around girls in the back of a van. He was no longer the tough guy who'd slapped me around. He was a scared boy, cowering to his mother's every command.

"Well, we can't leave him here. Go out to the shed and get a tarp. There's blood everywhere. We've got to roll him up before we move him."

Travis did what his mother said, and I was left alone with her again.

"I knew Zeke ever since we moved up here when I was in middle school," she said. "Shoot, must be going on fifty years. He was older, of course. Took my sister Mary to the prom. She died a few years back, my sister. Lung cancer. Now here's Zeke, dead as a doorknob."

"And you're still here," I said, my head spinning from the murder I'd witnessed. I'd never seen a dead body before and wondered if that's what I would look like after they killed me—just a bag of skin and bones.

She let out a little chuckle like she was surprised and amused at the same time. "You're right. I'm still here. It's a shame you won't be around for much longer. But I can't allow it, not after what you've seen."

What are you waiting for?

Death would have come as a relief. But no matter how much I felt like giving up, there was still some part of me that wanted to live. It burned inside me, right next to the rage and the desire to kill Travis. Now I wanted to kill his mother too.

Travis returned with the tarp, and they rolled the sheriff up into a tidy bundle.

"Help me get him up the stairs," said Henrietta.

"And then what?"

"Then we put him in his car, roll it off that cliff five miles down the road. Must be two or three-hundred feet down to the bottom. He'll be busted up so bad they'll think it was an accident—if they ever even find him."

"But mama, don't you think we oughta wait until after dark?"

She shook her head. "Can't risk it. What if someone wanders up the drive and sees his car parked outside? This way, if anyone knew he was stopping by, we can say he never came, and they'll think he crashed on his way."

Travis took a moment to consider. "That's smart, mama. Real smart. But what if someone sees me driving his patrol car?"

"Ain't too many folks on that road. You just sit real low in the seat, boy. Put his hat and glasses on and raise a hand in front of your face to wave if anyone passes. And Travis, be careful when you push the car over."

"Yes, mama. But how will I get back?"

"You got legs, don't you? But don't follow the road; someone's bound to see you that way. Come up the creek bed and cross through the woods back to the cabin."

I watched as they worked together, mother and son, to haul the sheriff's dead weight up the wooden steps. Then I heard the car pull out of the driveway and wondered if Henrietta would come back down and kill me herself.

She appeared a few minutes later with a mop and a big yellow bucket. "Bleach," she said. "That's the trick to cleaning up bloodstains. They can come in with those special cameras, you know? Blue lights or something. I saw it on one of those crime scene shows I like watching on Sunday nights. Comes in real handy at a time like this."

She made several passes with the mop, each time emptying the reddish water in the bucket and adding a fresh round of bleach. She didn't finish until the water in the bucket was clear.

"Gotta let the bleach sink in real good. Down into the cracks and crevices. Most people end up rushing the job and wind up missing a spot."

I had to give it to the crazy old woman. She certainly knew how to cover up a murder. Still, I clung to the hope that someone would come looking for the sheriff and find me before it was too late—before I was just another murder for Henrietta to cover up.

By the time Travis came back, it was nearly dark outside the window. Henrietta had gone upstairs to the kitchen for more tea while I sat looking at the place where the sheriff had breathed his last breath.

I wonder if he has grandkids.

I pushed the thought out of my mind as they both came slogging down the stairs. Travis' boots and pants were muddy, and there was a scratch on one cheek.

"It's time," said Henrietta. "You have to kill her now, son. She's already seen far too much."

"But mama—"

"Don't you 'but mama' me, boy. She's a liability. A risk. And if anyone wanders in and finds her like the poor sheriff did, she'll send us both to death row."

If I hadn't been so terrified, I would have had time to feel sorry for Travis. His mother was insane. Murderous even. It's no wonder he turned out the way he did.

"I won't do it."

"You should have thought about that before you went and kidnapped another one."

It's an odd thing, listening to two people deliberate your death as if you weren't in the room. I began to feel as if I was floating out of my body, watching the scene unfold as I hovered near the ceiling.

"But I love her, mama. She's the one."

"Oh, you stupid, silly boy. Do you really think she's ever going to love you back? Look at her, Travis. You've got her locked up in chains and pissing in a bucket."

I snapped back into my body with sudden clarity and knew exactly what I had to do. "I do love him," I said. "I love you, Travis. I want to be with you forever and always, like Liang and the princess."

His face lit up. "See, mama. She loves me too."

"She's only saying that so you won't kill her. Don't be fooled by some wretched little whore."

"She's wrong," I said. "She's wrong, Travis. I didn't see it before, but I love you now."

Henrietta turned to face me, rage spilling out of her narrowed eyes. "Shut up, whore! Nobody loves my son except for me."

Travis moved in between us. "Don't call her that! She's not a whore. She's my girlfriend."

His mother scoffed. "You know something? You're even dumber than you look."

His lips quivered, and I thought he might cry, but instead, he stiffened up and stood his ground.

"Fine," she said, stomping up the stairs. "If you won't do it, then I'll kill her myself."

She came back with another plastic grocery bag and pushed him aside with the same strength I'd seen when she moved on the sheriff. I screamed and thrashed at the chains as she forced the bag over my head and pulled it tight. Plastic sucked into my mouth and nose, and I couldn't breathe. I closed my eyes.

This is it. In another minute, this will all be over.

Then I heard a thud and her fingers loosened their grip around my neck. I tore the plastic bag off, and when I opened my eyes, I saw Travis standing with a bloody hammer in his hand. His mother was standing too, a look of bewilderment and disbelief plastered across her face.

She collapsed to the ground in slow motion, first falling to her knees before sliding onto her back, her legs splayed out at odd angles on both sides.

Travis crumpled to the ground beside her. "Oh, what have I done? I'm sorry, mama. I'm so sorry."

Then he raised the hammer again and brought it down on her face. Then again. And again. Blood splattered in all directions. He swung and swung until he toppled over in a pool of blood and sweat.

I reached for the bucket and retched. The room spun around me as I struggled to understand what had happened.

Two murders in the same day.

A son had killed his own mother. But I was alive, and even though it made me feel like a bad person, I was happy it was her and not me.

Travis sobbed beside her for a long time. I didn't dare move or speak. If it had been possible, I wouldn't have even breathed, waiting to see what would happen next.

Then he stood and dropped the hammer to the bloody floor. "I did it for you," he said. "See? I did it all for you."

TWENTY

He wrapped her up in a plastic tarp the same way he'd wrapped up the sheriff. Any emotion he'd shown before was gone. He didn't cry. He didn't smile. I studied his face for any clue about what he might be feeling, but there was nothing. Maybe he was shutting out all of the things he felt, a person gone numb. Or maybe he just didn't care.

He picked her up and draped her lifeless corpse over his shoulder—the good one—the one I hadn't stabbed. Then he tromped up the stairs, laboring beneath her weight, and disappeared for some time.

Only an hour before, his mother had mopped the floor clean. Now it was covered again with blood. Her blood. I knew I had to be patient and handle Travis carefully, or soon it would be covered with mine too.

My thoughts drifted back to the night I'd left Portland. I knew at the time I'd made a big decision that would change things forever. But never in my wildest dreams had I imagined that decision would bring me here.

He was still in a somber mood when he returned. He didn't speak as he mopped the floor and scrubbed her blood from the walls with a soapy brush. He was careful to clean up well, though not as careful as she had been. Then he emptied my bucket, rinsing it out and placing it beside me again with a fresh roll of toilet paper.

"Are you hungry?" He looked at me for the first time since he'd dropped the hammer to the floor beside his mother's smashed face.

Normally, it would have been impossible for me to eat after witnessing such a gory crime. But I was hungry and thought food might settle my knotted stomach. "Yes," I said, "I could eat."

I regretted my decision as soon as I heard him moving around upstairs in the kitchen. A terrible idea forced its way into my head.

What if he's cooking his own mother? What if he intends to feed her to me?

I was relieved when he reappeared with two plates of eggs, toast, and bacon. I sniffed the bacon carefully just to be sure and took a bite only when I was satisfied it was not Henrietta I would be eating.

He positioned his chair directly over the place where she had died, and we ate in silence. When we'd both cleared our plates, he carried them upstairs and returned moments later with two cups of coffee.

"Do you know the story of the Boy and His Mother?"

"No," I said. I wasn't in the mood for another one of his stories, but it would have been better than sitting around in awkward silence.

"You'll like it," he said.

I sipped my coffee and nodded.

"One day, a man is apprehended for stealing. What exactly he had stolen, the story doesn't say. But he was sentenced to death—they killed people for stealing back in those days—and he was led to the gallows to be hanged.

"As the crowd threw rotten vegetables and heckled the condemned man, he caught sight of his weeping mother. He asked his executioners if he might speak with her one last time. It was not an unreasonable final request, and so his mother was brought to the platform where the noose had already been strung around the man's neck.

"He told her to come closer so that he could whisper in her ear. When she leaned in close, he bit her ear off with his teeth and spit it upon the wooden planks of the gallows.

"The crowd was terrorized and took pity on the poor mother, who surely did not deserve such a horrible son. But the man spoke. 'Do not be deceived by my mother,' he said. 'When I was only a small boy, I stole a book and gave it to her. Had she whipped or chastised me then, rather than encouraging me to steal more and telling me my thefts would go unnoticed, I surely would not have grown into the man condemned to die before you today. Whatever guilt has arisen from my actions is as much the responsibility of a mother whose poor education left me deficient.'

"The crowd directed their scorn and rotten vegetables at the mother as she scurried away in shame. As for the man? He was hanged with a smile on his face, for at least some of his guilt had disappeared along with his miserable mother."

It was clear to me exactly what he was trying to say, and he looked at me like he wanted me to believe him. But I didn't believe him. As awful as his mother had been, he wasn't a little boy. He was a man. He was responsible for the choices he'd made.

"So? What do you think?"

I lied. "It's a very interesting story."

"Don't you get it?"

"Oh, yes. The poor man was only a product of his environment."

A smile spread across his face. "And in the end, he finds peace because he finally frees himself from his mother's bad influence."

"Are you free, Travis?"

"Yes," he said. "It was her all along. Don't you see? I'll never do a bad thing again, not with you by my side."

We both know that isn't true.

"I'm with you," I said. It was another lie. "I love you."

I wanted to ask him to take the chains off, but I thought it might seem like I was rushing him. I had him exactly where I wanted him. He believed I understood him. And I knew that deep down, even a monster like Travis longs to be understood.

"Prove it," he said.

"What?"

"If you really love me, then prove it." He pushed the chair back and took two steps toward me.

I wanted to pull back, but instead, I climbed to my feet, chains rattling, and moved closer to him. "How do I prove my love?"

"Kiss me."

I'd rather bite your ear off.

But biting his ear off would have only convinced him that his mother was the one who had been right. As much as the thought of kissing him repulsed me, I knew my survival and eventual freedom depended on it. Like an animal who chews its own foot off to escape a trap, I was prepared to sacrifice a part of myself to save the whole.

He leaned forward, and his lips met mine. My arms were behind me now, pulled backward by the chains. He brought his hands up to my face, the same hands that had killed his mother only a few short hours before, and caressed my cheeks and neck.

I was floating out of my body again, this time to a beach with a salt breeze in my face and the sun on my back. I didn't come back until it was over.

"You're amazing," he said. "I want to kiss you like that until the day I die."

Let's hope that day comes soon.

I struggled to keep my eyes open. I was exhausted from the events of the day, but I stayed awake long after he'd gone upstairs, and his footsteps stopped moving around the cabin. I could rest later. For now, I still had work to do.

I started by carving another line. Then I got to work on the bolt in the wall. I snapped the chain up and down and twisted the links against the bolt in each direction until my arms were too tired to continue. I'd almost given up for the night when the bolt began to wiggle.

It was a tiny movement, so minuscule it was almost imperceptible. I wondered if maybe I was just seeing things. Maybe the days and nights in the basement were playing games in my head. But when I traced my fingers along the base of the bolt, more concrete dust fell away to the floor.

It wasn't nearly enough wiggle room to pull the bolt free, not even close, but any progress was better than none.

It's going to take time. And time is the only thing I have.

I told myself I had to keep going. I refused to lose hope, no matter how many murders I might witness or the horrors Travis would inflict upon me. I went to bed that night, curled up between the scratchy blankets, with something almost resembling a smile on my face.

TWENTY-ONE

Travis called it our two-week anniversary. He'd come bouncing down the stairs with a huge smile on his face, boasting about the lasagna he carried and how he'd made the pasta layers from scratch.

"Took me two hours," he said.

We'd developed something of a routine in the days since he'd killed his mother. He would appear in the late morning with breakfast and return each night with dinner. Often, he'd tell me one of his unusual stories, or we'd play card games together until we ended each night with another kiss. Then when he'd finally gone off to bed, I carved my lines and worked on the bolt.

Tonight was no different. We ate the lasagna, and he told me a story. This time it was about three sisters who each sought a hand in marriage.

"Their father was a successful merchant and wished to attract the best suitors," he said. "And so he hung a golden ball outside their house as an offer of marriage.

"A passing prince saw the golden ball and married the oldest daughter. So the father hung another ball, and soon thereafter married his second daughter to another prince.

"It was his youngest daughter's turn, but the father had spent all of his wealth on the first two and had no money left for another golden ball.

"Instead, the youngest daughter was married off to a peasant, a young man who she'd loved since they'd played in the fields together as children. The older sisters looked down on the younger sister's poverty and refused to be seen with her.

"Many years passed. The oldest sister's princely husband squandered his fortune before dying in a foreign war. The second sister's husband lost his money to gambling debts and ran away with another woman, leaving her to face the creditors alone.

"But the youngest daughter's peasant husband saved his meager earnings and became an even wealthier merchant than her father had been. And even though they had treated her with disdain, she took pity on her older sisters and cared for them in their old age. She and her husband lived happily ever after because their marriage had been one of true love."

I scraped at the remaining lasagna on my plate and wondered if anyone was even still looking for me. I was a criminal as far as they were concerned—just another mugshot on a wanted list.

"Do you love me, Spencer? Do you really love me?"

"Huh?" I had been too lost in thought to consider his question or how it might relate to the story.

"Were you even paying attention?"

"I'm sorry, Travis. It was a really wonderful story."

His face turned sour. "Sometimes, I don't think you really love me. I can feel it when we kiss. You never look me in the eyes. It's like you go somewhere else."

It had been a mistake, not paying attention. "I love you, Travis. I promise."

"You're lying!" He flipped the plate from my hands, and it smashed to pieces on the floor. "I worked so hard on the lasagna, and now it's ruined. You ruined our anniversary. Maybe mama was right. Maybe you've been lying all along."

I'd seen him flip from hot to cold before and knew how dangerous it could be. His emotions were getting out of hand, and I had to think fast before things got any worse.

He jumped to his feet and paced back and forth. "It's Stockholm syndrome. I saw a television show about it once."

"Stockholm what?"

"Stockholm syndrome. It's when hostages or captives develop feelings of sympathy and sometimes even love for their captors. But it's not real, Spencer." His face turned red, and he started to cry. "None of this is real."

I'm losing him.

I'd worked too hard to build up his trust. If I lost it now, it could take weeks or even months to get it back. And I needed his trust if my plans for escape had any chance of working.

It's time. I can't wait any longer.

"Come here," I said, opening my arms wide. "Let me show you how I love you."

He collapsed into my arms, and I pulled him closer. His body trembled as I held his crying face against my breast the way a mother cradles a child.

"Quiet now," I said. "It's okay, Travis. Everything is going to be okay."

"Don't ever leave me, Spencer."

"No, I won't ever leave you."

I held him until he stopped trembling, then I lifted his face from my breast and stroked his cheek. My hand followed his neck down to his shirt and began to open the buttons.

He reached up to stop me. "Spencer—"

"Don't you want it?"

"Yes," he said. "I want it."

I finished with the buttons and moved down to his pants. He was already hard.

We went to the floor together. His hot breath warmed my skin as I unbuttoned my own pants and slid them down around my knees.

And then he was inside me. I was tempted to float away, back to my spot near the ceiling where I could watch what was happening instead of living it. But I forced myself to remain present. I had to be ready when the moment finally came.

He moaned my name.

"Yes, baby?"

"I love you," he said.

"I love you too."

His muscles tensed, and his breathing quickened. It was almost time. Time to end this nightmare.

My fingers found a piece of the broken plate and wrapped themselves around it. I aimed for his neck and swung as hard as I could.

Missed.

The shard buried itself deep into his upper arm, the same one I'd stabbed in the shoulder with the knife. Travis pulled back and cried out in pain.

But I didn't wait. I raised my hands above my head and pulled at the chains around my wrists. The bolt came free of the wall with a glorious pop.

Travis was too busy pulling the shard from his arm to notice me roll behind him. I came up with the chain in both hands and wrapped it around his neck.

He struggled against my grip, but I held tight. It was a fight only one of us would win, and I'd already decided the winner would be me.

Little by little, he weakened. He, too, grabbed a broken piece of the plate and swung at me. But it was a wild swing, and he missed.

I pulled the chain harder until his face turned blue. My hands were bleeding, but it didn't matter. The adrenaline surged through me, and I hardly noticed the pain.

He made one last attempt to break free, the pathetic efforts of a sad and dying man. Then the fight left him, and his body went completely limp.

Quick. Find the keys.

I didn't want to touch him. He was so ugly lying there with his naked midsection, exposed as the monster that he really was. But I dug through his pockets until I found the key to the shackles.

Steady. Breathe.

My hands shook so hard I dropped the key once or twice, but in another minute, my ankles were free. Then I raced up the stairs in search of the wrench he'd used to tighten the cuffs that still hung from my wrists.

I tore apart every cabinet and cupboard in the kitchen. There were knives and screwdrivers and the bottle opener he'd used the night we drank the wine, but no wrench.

There wasn't much in the living room besides the old sofa, so I moved to the back of the cabin, to the room I'd never seen in my time upstairs. It was his bedroom.

By all accounts, it was ordinary. A bed with neatly tucked sheets. A dresser. I pulled the drawers apart in my search for the wrench, but they held nothing but folded pants and rolled pairs of socks.

The closet door creaked as I swung it open. Shirts hung in a tidy row. I rifled through them, then felt my hand along the top shelf until I found a box.

Inside were Polaroid pictures of sleeping girls, chained up in the basement the same as I had been. I counted three, no four, separate faces, and wondered how many girls had died alone in his dungeon. How many families had cried themselves to sleep at night wondering what had happened to their daughters?

As cruel as it might have been, I had no time for sympathy. That would come later. I returned the box to the shelf and continued my search for the wrench.

Maybe it's in the basement.

I tiptoed back to the basement door and peered down the stairs. I didn't want to go back down there, not after everything I'd been through. But I needed the wrench to free myself of the chains. I had to be brave.

My foot found the first step. Then the second.

My eyes moved to the corner where I'd killed him and left his body to rot. It was empty. Travis was gone.

TWENTY-TWO

"Looking for this?" The voice came from behind me.

I spun around just in time to see Travis standing in the doorway. He swung the wrench at my head, and I ducked, grabbing his arm and pulling him down the stairs.

He tumbled to the bottom in a mess of arms and legs. "You bitch! I'll fucking kill you!"

And so I ran, my heart beating wildly in my chest, out of the front door and into the cool night air.

He's right behind me. Think, Spencer. Think.

I tried the door of his truck, but it was locked. I spun in all directions, hoping to see something, anything. There was a shed to one side of the cabin. I thought maybe there might be something inside I could use as a weapon. I ran toward it as fast as my feet could carry me.

He emerged from the cabin just as soon as I reached the shed. It wouldn't be long before he closed the distance. I held my breath as I grabbed the door handle and turned.

It was unlocked, and the door swung open.

The inside was dark. My hands fumbled around in the darkness until I found a light switch and flicked it on. Rows of garden tools lined one wall—rusty hoes and hedge trimmers and shovels.

A large meat freezer lined the opposite wall. I dug my heels in as I pushed it in front of the door only seconds before he tried forcing his way in.

It won't hold him long.

He slammed his weight against the door, and the lid of the meat freezer flipped open. Henrietta's mangled and frozen face stared back at me, her body twisted up with her legs on either side of her head.

That's when I remembered what she had told the sheriff moments before she killed him.

"We have a shotgun," she had said. But if it was true, my search of the cabin had turned up empty.

Travis slammed his weight against the door again. It would only be another minute or two until he finally forced his way inside.

Whether by some unknown instinct or miracle, I looked up and saw an old, double-barreled shotgun on a rack above the doorway. I shut the lid of the freezer and climbed on top, took the shotgun in my hands. The wooden stock felt smooth, no doubt worn down by many hands throughout the years.

Shells. I need shotgun shells.

A year before I met Matt, I'd gone on a few dates with a soldier recently returned from a tour in Iraq, whose idea of a romantic time was a trip to the gun range. I thought it was silly then, but as I cradled the shotgun in my hands, I was grateful I'd learned to use one, even if I hadn't ever been much of a good shot.

My thumb found the lever on top and the side-by-side barrels pivoted away from the stock. There were two shells, one in each barrel, though I wondered how long they had been there and if they would even fire.

No time. It's the best I've got.

I backed myself into the corner of the shed just as the door finally swung open.

Point and squeeze.

The barrel exploded in a flash of light. Travis staggered backward, still clutching the wrench in his hand.

I'll never forget the look in his eyes as he fell to the ground. It was surprise—the same look on his mother's face when he swung the hammer into her head.

Then everything was silent, except for the chirping of crickets and the hooting of the owl in the distance.

The road wound its way down a canyon. I'd found his truck keys on a hook in the kitchen and left him there, blood oozing from his chest, as I fired up the engine and started down the long gravel drive.

My hands still shook as I navigated the truck around the twists and bends of the road. It wasn't until I reached I-70, more than eighty miles from where I'd left Travis to die, that my muscles relaxed, and I began to breathe normally.

In another thirty minutes, I crossed the state border.

A sign read: LEAVING COLORFUL COLORADO. COME BACK SOON.

Colorado. All this time, I was in Colorado.

I could have stopped at any of the small towns along the way and found the local police station. I could have told them my story, about what had happened with Travis in the cabin deep in the Colorado mountains. But I was still a wanted fugitive. I wondered if they'd even believe me or simply stuff me in the back of another transport van. That was a place I never wanted to find myself again. So I pushed on. I had unfinished business in Oregon—unfinished business with Matt.

I followed I-70 west to Green River, where the unnamed girl had cried and pissed herself in the seat. At the time, I'd felt sorry for her, considering the threats Travis had made.

Good girls live. Bad girls die.

But she had been the lucky one.

At Green River, I followed the signs and US-191 north toward Salt Lake City. I drove through the night, stopping only once to pee on the side of the road.

I passed a ghost town and the abandoned gas station at Woodside and had just cleared Wellington when the engine sputtered, and the truck ran out of gas.

The sun was breaking over the horizon as I stuck out my thumb and hoped for a ride. There wasn't much traffic, but it wasn't long before a semi-truck pulled over, and the driver motioned for me to get in.

"Where you headed?"

"Portland."

"Ain't going to Portland," he said. "But I can get you as far as Boise."

All I knew was that he seemed friendly, and Boise was a long way from the cabin in Colorado.

He eyed me suspiciously as I climbed into the cab. "You just gonna leave your pickup?"

"It's not mine," I said.

"Well, alright then. Ain't none of my business anyway. Say, you okay?"

"Better now. Thank you."

He caught me staring at a photo of him taped to the dashboard. His arm was around a woman about his age, and between them stood a young girl in a t-shirt.

"My pride and joy," he said. "That's my wife, Linda. And the girl you see in the middle is my daughter. Of course, I don't see them as much as I'd like, on account of being out on the road. But everything I do is for them."

"They look nice."

"Sure are. Hey, I didn't get your name."

"It's Spencer," I said.

"Well, Spencer, my name is Jim, but just about everyone calls me Jimbo. You can do the same if you like."

I almost didn't hear what he'd said. I was too absorbed by the picture of him and his family. They looked so happy and normal, so far away from the hell I'd lived through in the past two weeks.

I'd resolved to keep my guard up, but there in the cab of Jimbo's truck, as we hurtled down the road at seventy miles an hour, I finally broke down and cried.

"Go on," he said. "Don't hold back. You look like you could use a good cry."

"Thank you," I said through tears.

"Ain't no need for thanks. You rest now, Spencer. Let ol' Jimbo take care of everything."

And so I slept—a deep, dreamless sleep. When I woke, he was touching me gently on the shoulder. A sign outside the window announced our arrival in Boise.

Despite the size of his semi-truck, Jimbo insisted on taking me all the way to the bus station in the center of town. "You got money?"

"It's okay," I said. "I'll figure something out."

He reached into his back pocket and pulled out his wallet, handed me two crisp, hundred dollar bills. "That oughta get you to Portland."

"I can't, Jim."

"Now, don't you say no. It ain't charity, and I know you ain't asking. Just consider it a little help, from one friend to another."

I took the money and thanked him.

"Say, Spencer?"

"Yes?"

"I know it ain't none of my business, but if anyone did to my daughter what it looks like someone did to you, I'd kill them with my own two hands."

"You're a good man," I said. "She's lucky to have you."

Even though I'd slept most of the day in the cab of Jimbo's truck, I fell asleep as soon as the bus crossed the Oregon state line.

We arrived in Portland at eleven o'clock at night. I hailed a cab from the bus station and gave the driver Matt's address—my address too, not so long ago.

The driveway was empty. I went around to the side of the garage and peered in through a window. The garage was empty too. Maybe it was because his Audi was still totaled in an impound lot in Topeka. But I knew Matt, and I was sure he would have already bought a new one. He wasn't the type to take public transportation.

He was probably out with friends, celebrating another big real estate deal and laughing about his crazy ex-girlfriend rotting away in a jail cell somewhere.

The key was under a plastic rock by the front porch, the same place he always left it. And the code for the security system hadn't changed: 0413—his birthday.

I took a seat on the living room sofa and waited for him in the dark. It was two hours past midnight when I finally heard the garage door roll open.

TWENTY-THREE

"Spencer?" He dropped the styrofoam takeout container he'd been carrying when he flicked on the light and found me sitting on the couch. "What are you doing here?"

"Take a seat," I said. "We need to talk."

"I'm calling the police. They're looking for you, something about a transport van going missing and two bodies found in separate states. A detective came by the house and asked me a bunch of questions."

Two bodies? So they'd found Ruby too.

"Put down the phone, Matt. You're going to sit and listen to what I have to say."

I was prepared to knock the phone out of his hands, but he returned it to his pocket and took a seat opposite me on a cushioned leather chair.

"Did you kill them?"

"No, I didn't kill them. It was the driver of the van. He kidnapped me and held me for two weeks in the basement of his cabin. He killed his own mother too."

"Jesus." He rubbed at his temples. It was hard for someone with Matt's limited imagination to process what I was telling him. "Did you call the police?"

"I'll tell them everything in the morning. And you will too, Matt. You're going to tell them everything."

"Me? What do I have to say?"

"Let's start with the car. You're going to tell them it was all a mistake. Your mistake. And you're going to insist they drop the charges."

"Gee, Spencer. It's a little more complicated than that."

I ignored him. "Then you're going to tell them I never tried to kill you. I'd only acted in self-defense."

"Now hold on a minute. Self-defense? But I never did anything other than care for you."

"Matt, you held my face under the water in the bathtub and told me you'd kill me if I didn't stop going out with my friends. And then, when I tried to leave, you grabbed me around the neck. After the things I've seen and done, believe me, smashing a model home over your head hardly adds up to attempted murder."

"I won't do it."

"You will, first thing in the morning."

"But they'll arrest me, Spencer. It'll ruin my career. I'm sure we can work something else out. Do you want money? I'll give you money, and you can go away. We can forget about everything. Please, I don't want to go to jail. I can't go to jail."

As I watched him plead with me, I thought about the person I used to be only a few short weeks ago. I would have caved to his demands. I would have let him bully me into going along with whatever he wanted, convinced it was best for both of us.

But now he was nothing more than a desperate little boy, still believing he could avoid the consequences of what he'd done. The fear I'd felt that night as I took his car and fled across five states was gone. I'd survived much worse than Matt, the real estate agent.

"I don't care," I said. "I don't care about your career or the money. I want my life back, and I'm going to take it."

"But—"

"No more talking. Go upstairs and get some rest. You're going to need it in the morning."

He looked at me like he was seeing me for the very first time. The pleasing girl he'd controlled for six months was gone, replaced by something harder and stronger.

Then I saw something flash in his eyes I now recognized easily. It was surprise and fear.

He stood and headed for the stairs, his shoulders slumped in defeat. "What are you going to do?"

"Me? I'm going to stay right here and drink some of the gourmet coffee you have in the kitchen. I don't want you getting cold feet and running off."

"Whatever."

"I'll see you in the morning, Matt. Sweat dreams."

It was nine o'clock sharp when Matt followed the detectives into a briefing room at the central Portland police station. I watched him go, and sipped cheap coffee with a stale danish from the vending machine.

Two hours later, the detectives came for me. I sat across from them in a paneled room, much the same as I'd sat across from the lawyer in Topeka. In between us, on the center of the table, was a recording device. One of the detectives leaned forward and switched it on.

"Ms. Madison, I'm Detective Jeffries, and my partner here is Sergeant Kowalski. Can we get you anything? More coffee? A soda, maybe?"

I shook my head.

"Well," he said. "It seems there have been some new developments in the attempted murder case. Your fiancé admitted to threatening your life. We'll be making a formal recommendation to the district attorney's office to drop all of the charges against you. As for your fiancé, he's been taken into custody on charges of domestic violence, verbal threats, and filing a false police report. And if you'd like, we can provide a victim's advocate who will assist you with filing a restraining order and obtaining any assets you held jointly with Matt."

"That won't be necessary." Matt had already agreed to hand over half the money in our bank account on the way to the police station.

The detective shifted in his chair. "Now, there's still the matter of what happened in that van. There's an FBI agent waiting outside to take your statement. Are you sure you don't want anything? We might be here a while."

"I'm fine."

"Well, alright then." He left the room and came back a moment later with the agent. "Ms. Madison, this is Special Agent Rodriguez with the Federal Bureau of Investigation."

She held out her hand. "Please, call me Isabel. Do you mind if I call you Spencer?"

"I would prefer it."

She smiled as she placed her own recording device on the table. "Great. Now, why don't you tell me everything that happened out there?"

"Where do I start?"

"At the beginning," she said. "Start at the beginning."

So I told her about the long trip in the van, about the stupid milkshake and the strange phone calls and Monica disappearing in the middle of the night. I told her about waking up in his basement. The violence. The psychological torture. I told her about the sheriff, and Henrietta, and how Travis had killed her too. I told her about the photos in the closet and gave her the bloody tooth. And I told her about my escape.

She listened intently, never interrupting or asking a single question. She only looked away to scratch notes in her pad.

When it was finished, I took a long breath and sunk back into my seat. "Detective Jeffries, could I please have that soda now?"

"After that story, you can have anything you want."

Isabel waited until I'd had a drink and a quick bathroom break before continuing the interview. "So, Travis is dead?"

"I shot him in the chest with a shotgun, if that's what you mean. He looked dead."

"And this hunting cabin, he mentioned it belonged to his uncle?"

"That's what he told me, but I don't know if it's true."

"Thank you, Spencer. This has all been very helpful. I'll get in touch with the Colorado field office, and we'll have agents out there by nightfall. If what you said about the box of photos is true, it may help us connect Travis to several other missing women. On a personal note, I'd just like to say you've been incredibly brave."

Detective Jeffries escorted me out of the station. "Here's my card," he said. "If you need anything, don't hesitate to call me. Day or night, it doesn't matter."

Six hours after I'd walked into the police station with Matt, it was over. He was in custody. Soon they'd find Travis and his mother. The things I'd seen and experienced would never go away. But I was a survivor, prepared for wherever the future would take me.

TWENTY-FOUR

"So, he just buried them behind the cabin?" Felicity sipped a cappuccino as she sat across from me in a little seaside coffee house.

We'd reconnected in the months since I'd been back in Portland and had driven out together to our favorite spot on the Pacific Coast.

I pulled my black hoodie around my shoulders. "Yeah, that's what Isabel said."

A forensic team had found a total of six bodies buried in the woods behind the cabin, all young women who had been reported missing, plus Henrietta still folded up in the meat freezer. But most importantly, Travis had died from a shotgun wound exactly where I'd left him.

"I'm sorry, Spencer. We don't have to talk about it if you don't want to."

"No, it's okay. I think it's better. Talking about it helps me get it off my chest."

"Speaking of talking about it?"

"The book deal?"

"Yes, the book deal. Are you going to take it? It's a lot of money, Spencer. And Marianne Dixon is such a wonderful author. I'm sure she'd do your story justice."

It was a lot of money. The publisher had offered half a million dollars for the rights to my story, enough money to start a new life. But I didn't need it. When word hit the press about what had happened to me, Correctional Transport Company of America had been quick to offer a multi-million dollar settlement.

"I'm going to pass on the book deal."

"Really?"

"I've been thinking about it a lot, and I've decided to write the book myself. There's a memoir writing workshop at Portland State. Who knows? Maybe it'll lead to other things."

Felicity looked at me over her raised coffee cup and scrunched up her nose. "Spencer Madison, you're such a badass. And for the record, I'm expecting a signed copy."

"Sure thing, Felicity. Sure thing."

We strolled along the beach and talked. Felicity was full of questions about the future—questions about what I was going to do with the money.

I didn't have many answers. I'd barely had time to think, not with finding a new place to live, the settlement arrangements, and a half-dozen follow-up interviews with the FBI. I'd even tracked down Jimbo the trucker and offered to pay him back a hundredfold.

He'd answered my call with the enthusiasm of a long lost relative but had been quick to turn down my offer.

"I told you," he'd said in his casual way. "Just one friend helping out another."

After some pressure, he'd finally agreed to let me establish a college fund for his daughter, but only after I'd promised to attend her graduation. I still thought about him often.

Felicity stopped walking and put her hand on my shoulder. "Silly me, I've been blabbering away for hours. Are you doing okay? You seemed a bit lost there."

"It's all so weird, Felicity."

"Weird?" She cocked her head to one side. "I'm not sure I understand. But if you want to talk, I'll listen."

"Look around." I motioned toward two young children and a spotted mutt—a boy and his sister playing and splashing where the waves sputtered out on the sand. "It's so normal. Everything is just so normal."

"That's good, right?"

"I guess. But I don't feel normal. I try not to be angry or resent people going about their happy lives, unaware of the horrors others live through. But sometimes I feel like I'm in a different place. Maybe it's what soldiers experience when they come back from a war. In their heads, it's still battles and bullets, but everyone else is eating ice cream."

"What does your therapist say?"

"She says it's going to take a while. I have to be patient and work through it." I sighed. "Some days are better than others."

"How are you sleeping?"

"Just fine." It was true. I'd been sleeping through most nights like a log. There were no more nightmares of wooden boxes or deep lakes.

She put her hand on my shoulder again. "I'm always here for you if you need anything. Hey, how about another cup of coffee? That always lifts my spirits."

"Actually, if it's okay with you, I'd like to be alone for a little while."

She smiled. "I understand. No problem at all. Meet you back at the hotel at seven?"

I watched her meander toward the hotel and then continued down the beach alone.

The sun was sinking lower in the west, staining the shimmering waves in pink and purple hues. In the distance, a lone rock rose up a hundred feet out of the water, standing in defiance of the unrelenting Pacific.

I closed my eyes and imagined I was that rock. Waves pummeled against me without end. But still, I stood.

Just breathe.

It was something I'd told myself often while locked away in the basement. It had served me well, always pulling me back to the present moment and quieting my spinning thoughts.

Breathe.

I stood on the beach for a long time, gazing out over the waves until the sun had sunk beneath the horizon and disappeared from sight.

Then I gathered myself up and headed back along the beach toward the hotel. It was late, and Felicity would be waiting for me. In the morning, we'd return to the city with its hustle and bustle—the endless demands. But for the first time in many months, I allowed myself to feel free.

There was only one thing left to do.

TWENTY-FIVE

It was late fall when I loaded up my Honda Fit and headed east on I-84. I'd purchased the car with the settlement money I'd received from Correctional Transport Company of America. It wasn't fancy like Matt's Audi, but it was mine.

Portland was behind me in an hour, the congestion of the city giving way to red and yellow forests on either side of the road. I munched on snacks and watched the scenery pass outside the window.

The highway wound its way along the Columbia River and the border of Washington and Oregon. I followed it to the junction of I-90, then headed northeast, in the direction of Spokane.

There was plenty of time to think about things out there on the road. It had been six weeks since I'd gone to the beach with Felicity, and with each day, I felt a slow return to my old self.

I'd even enrolled in the memoir workshop at Portland State and was making progress on my story. It felt good putting it all down in writing, as if by transferring my words to the page, I was finally leaving it behind me.

Maybe soon I'll go a whole day without thinking about Travis.

I reached Spokane in five and a half hours, pulling off the road for a brief detour to a flower shop. The kind old woman behind the counter asked me the occasion.

"I'm not sure," I said.

"Baby shower? Wedding?"

"Um, none of the above."

"Well, what are you looking for, dear?"

I hadn't thought about it much. "Something bright, I guess."

She showed me a bouquet of yellow daffodils, and I decided it was perfect. Its delicate fragrance filled the car as I headed west out of Spokane toward the little town of Moses Lake.

The GPS on my phone guided me to the place I'd been looking for. It wasn't much more than a grassy field a few miles outside of town. A man at the gate gave me a map, and I continued on foot past row after row of marble and granite headstones.

I'd prepared myself well for the moment, but when I saw her name carved in red sandstone, I fell to my knees and cried.

HERE LIES RUBY ELIZABETH MONTGOMERY, BELOVED SISTER AND GRANDDAUGHTER. REST IN PEACE.

"I'm sorry," I said. "I'm so sorry, I couldn't save you."

Silence.

Then I saw her smiling face, and heard her laugh, felt her head resting gently on my shoulder. "It's okay, Spencer. Everything is going to be okay."

I stayed there for a long time. When I finally got back to the car, 'I Will Survive' was playing on the radio. I turned it up as I pulled out of the gravel parking lot and headed back to Portland, laughing and crying and singing along with the words. And I knew they were true.

AUTHOR'S NOTE

You Are Mine is a tough story about a young woman who learns to believe in herself despite impossible odds. While it's a short book (as far as novels go), I can't say it was easy to write.

Spencer endures some authentic horrors and challenges on her long road to freedom, and I felt them with every keystroke.

In the end, I fell in love with Spencer and the incredible resolve with which she overcomes seemingly impossible circumstances. As a reader, I hope you've come to appreciate her story as much as I have.

If this is your first time reading one of my books, thank you for giving it a go. Please consider leaving your honest feedback in the form of a review. I take the time to read each and every one of them.

For those of you who are returning readers (you know who you are), I extend my deepest gratitude. Without readers like you, there would be no stories to tell.

And so we've reached the end. This is the place where I'm supposed to sucker you into joining my mailing list with the offer of some free, bogus book.

But I'm not going to do that. I hate junk emails as much as you do. Instead, I offer newsletter subscribers the chance to review advance copies, and I promise to only send emails when I have something important to say (most often whenever I publish a new book).

If I haven't scared you away, and you still want to subscribe, head over to my website at rickyfry.com.

Wishing you all the best,

Ricky
Tbilisi, Georgia
October 15th, 2020

READ NEXT

Nancy Hardaway was in bed, propped against a pillow with the latest Vanity Fair clutched in her pencil-thin fingers, when she was startled by a loud thump coming from Baby Nora's nursery. She lowered the magazine to her lap and nudged her sleeping husband.

"Byron," she said, "something isn't right in the nursery. Go and see what's happened."

Mr. Hardaway groaned and rolled over beneath the heavy comforter. "It's probably just the nanny, my love. Maybe she dropped something."

Whatever the nanny dropped must have been very heavy to make such a terrible noise. Just once, she thought, it would be nice to have a proper night's sleep. Baby Nora had been nothing but trouble since they brought her home from Massachusetts General Hospital. It had only been six months, but Nancy Hardaway was thoroughly exhausted.

The nanny was supposed to make life easier. Compared to most first-time mothers, Nancy had taken a decidedly hands-off role in the raising of their daughter. She'd stopped breast-feeding the moment Nora's first teeth had appeared, pumping milk with an expensive device and switching to formula not long after. It was an easy decision. She couldn't stand the way Nora chewed and bit her nipples.

Tonight she was especially tired, and had hoped to get some rest before the charity fundraiser she'd be attending with Mr. Hardaway the following evening. The high society ladies could be so judgmental, and she didn't dare show her face without at least eight hours of beauty sleep. The years had been kind to her, but still, she wasn't getting any younger. After nearly a decade of trying with no luck, Baby Nora was a surprise. The last thing Nancy Hardaway had expected was to become a mother on the eve of her thirty-seventh birthday.

She listened again for any sign of the nanny stirring in the nursery, but there was only silence. She thought there should at least be footsteps, the sound of the young but plump nanny passing through the corridor on the way back to her room. And Nora—there had never been a baby who cried as often as Nora. Such a disturbance would certainly have woken her.

Thank goodness the sleeping pill she'd taken before settling in with her magazine had yet to work its modern magic. Just a quick check of the nursery and she'd be drifting off to sleep in a matter of minutes. She had an especially big day tomorrow. Though there were few things she loved more than socializing at charity events, they were always so much trouble.

She felt her way along the corridor in the dark, until she found the switch. The long hall was empty, the nursery to one side and the nanny's room opposite. The nanny's door was open. Nancy leaned over the threshold and peered inside. The light beside the bed was still on but there was no sign of the young woman. Perhaps, she thought, she was still in the nursery tending to Nora.

She stopped to listen outside the nursery door. It was strange, the old house being so quiet. The door creaked as she pushed it open and a chill ran down her spine. In the faint glow of an old table lamp, she saw a plump figure spread on the floor beside the crib. The twisted face of the nanny stared up at her, a look of horror frozen in her motionless eyes.

Nancy Hardaway screamed. She'd never seen a dead body in real life before, but the young nanny certainly looked very dead. A slight trickle of blood oozed from the lifeless woman's mouth and pooled on the hardwood floor beneath her.

"What is it, Nancy?" Mr. Hardaway appeared in the doorway with a golf club in his hand.

"She's dead, Byron. She's dead." It was the only thing she could think to say.

"Call 9-1-1." He knelt beside the bleeding woman and shook her limp body, called her by a first name his wife had never once used during the nanny's short time in their employ.

Nancy couldn't move. She couldn't think. As she watched her husband pumping up and down on the young woman's chest, the only thing that filled the panicked space of her mind was the loud thump that had surely been the woman's body as she keeled over on the hardwood floor.

And there, in the crib at the center of the room, Baby Nora smiled up at her—a tiny bundle wrapped in swaddling blankets—with a peculiar look of satisfaction on her glowing, angelic face.

It was only later, long after the flashing lights and siren of the ambulance had pulled away from the Federalist façade of their Beacon Hill townhouse, that the Hardaways learned their daughter's nanny was indeed quite dead. They'd have to wait for the official report, of course, but the investigator from the medical examiner's office said it appeared as though she'd died of a sudden brain hemorrhage. "It's quite rare," he told them, "for someone of such a young age."

"Oh, dear." Nancy thought it was terrible. She wondered what the other society women would say. As far as she could recall, no one had ever lost a nanny before, with the exception of the McDowell's nanny, who'd died in her sleep. But the tough old Scottish woman had been seventy-nine, long overdue for retirement. Such things happen, and nobody had faulted Lisa McDowell.

"We've been unable to locate her family," said the investigator. "Perhaps you have their contact information, or at least something we might find useful?"

She was almost ashamed to admit she knew so little of the woman who'd spent the previous three months sleeping under their roof. "I'm sorry. I was never very good about those things."

"I see." He scratched his chin and scribbled notes in a little pad. "Did she ever mention anything to you about her state of health?"

"What do you mean?" Nancy had always just assumed the young woman was perfectly normal, if not slightly overweight.

"Was she unwell? Did she say anything or visit a doctor?" He'd already searched the nanny's room for any signs of a health condition and had found nothing, not even a bottle of aspirin.

Nancy still wasn't thinking clearly after such a distressing incident, but she recalled a conversation they'd had in the kitchen one morning while Inez, the Hardaway's long-time housekeeper, prepared breakfast. It was difficult to forget the look of fear that had gripped the young woman's face.

"She'd complained of having frequent nightmares—such terrible nightmares."

The investigator didn't look up as he continued writing in his notepad. "What sort of nightmares?"

"She wouldn't mention specifics." It was true. The nanny had been reluctant to describe the nature of her terrifying nighttime visions. "She'd wake in a fright. I heard her screaming from our bedroom down the hall."

"Interesting." He scratched his chin again. "I'm not sure it has anything to do with a brain hemorrhage, but we appreciate any details you can provide."

"Of course." She'd considered firing the nanny on more than one occasion—on the nights when she'd been woken by the woman's screams. Nora's frequent crying was bad enough. Her husband had convinced her otherwise, if only to save themselves the trouble of finding a new nanny. But a new nanny was now exactly what they needed.

The investigator finished taking notes and they were left alone in the quiet space of the house. Nora was sound asleep. Nancy, whose sleeping pill had finally taken effect, was utterly exhausted from their ordeal.

It was nearly morning. The high society ladies of Boston would surely notice her absence at the charity event, but it would be even worse to explain the sudden death of their nanny. She imagined their faces—wrinkles smoothed over by Botox injections—as they feigned sympathy, each secretly delighted it hadn't happened to them.

"Oh, Byron." She rested a hand on her husband's broad shoulder. "This has all been so dreadful. What am I going to tell the ladies?"

"It could be worse."

"How could things possibly be worse than this?"

"Just think," he said. "At least you're not the nanny."

He Comes in the Night, a supernatural horror novel by Ricky Fry, is available from Amazon in Kindle and paperback editions, or wherever fine books are sold.